How & Why STORIES
World Tales Kids Can Read & Tell

Martha Hamilton and Mitch Weiss
Beauty and the Beast Storytellers

Illustrations by Carol Lyon

August House Publishers, Inc.
LITTLE ROCK

Printed in the United States of America
10 9 8 7 6 5 4 3 2 1   HC
10 9 8 7 6 5 4 3 2 1   PB

LIBRARY OF CONGRESS CATALOGING-IN-PUBLICATION DATA
How & why stories : world tales kids can read & tell /
Martha Hamilton and Mitch Weiss ; illustrations by Carol Lyon.
p.   cm.
Summary: A collection of twenty-five traditional stories explaining why an
animal or plant or natural object looks or acts the way it does. Following each story are
storytelling tips and short modern, scientific explanations for the subject of the story.
ISBN 0–87483–562–3 (hardcover : alk. paper). --
ISBN 0–87483–561–5 (paperback : alk. paper)
1. Tales. [1. Folklore. 2. Storytelling Collections.]
I. Hamilton, Martha. II. Weiss, Mitch. III. Lyon, Carol, 1963– ill.
IV. Title: How and why stories.
PZ8. 1.H8645   1999
398.2--dc21   99-34953
CIP

Executive Editor: Liz Parkhurst
Copy Editor: Tom Baskett, Jr.
Project Editor: Joy Freeman
Cover and Interior Illustration: Carol Lyon
Cover and Book Design: Joy Freeman

AUGUST HOUSE, INC.   PUBLISHERS   LITTLE ROCK

Acknowledgments

We give warm thanks to those who read the manuscript and offered suggestions: Karen Baum, Marty Kaminsky, and June Locke. Thanks also to Joe Bruchac, Lee-Ellen Marvin and Margaret Read MacDonald, who answered our questions and helped solve some thorny problems; to Nancy Skipper, Janet McCue, and Bob Kibbee, who are invaluable for their library know-how and deep friendships that have endured (even though Martha has long been a "lapsed" librarian); to the Inter-Library Loan Department at Tompkins County Public Library, which managed to locate and borrow just about every obscure, antiquated book we requested; to the many teachers, principals, librarians, and parents who hire us year after year, allowing us to do what we do; to the New York State Council on the Arts and the New York Foundation for the Arts for helping fund many of our residencies; to Liz Parkhurst for her initial interest in the project and her guidance throughout; to Joy Freeman, Tom Baskett, Jr., and all the other great folks at August House for making this book a reality; to our good friends and family, who have supported us and endured, with patience and humor, through the writing of this book; and, of course, to the kids, whose courage and enthusiasm make the stories shine. Thanks for making it all possible.

Permissions

Contents

Introduction 10

Where the Stories Come From (Map) 12

How and Why Stories

Thunder and Lightning 15
    Nigeria (Ibibio)

How Tigers Got Their Stripes 18
    Vietnam

Why Bat Flies Alone At Night 21
    U.S. (Modoc Indian)

The Mill at the Bottom of the Sea .23
    Korea

Why Cats Wash Their Paws After Eating 26
    Europe

Why Ants Are Found Everywhere 28
    Burma

Why Frog and Snake Never Play Together 30
    Cameroon/Nigeria (Ekoi)

Why the Baby Says "Goo" 33
    U.S. (Penobscot Indian)

Why the Farmer and the Bear Are Enemies 36
    Russia

Why Hens Scratch in the Dirt 38
    Philippines

Why the Sun Comes Up When Rooster Crows 41
    China

Why Dogs Chase Cats 44
    U.S. (African-American)

The Dancing Brothers 46
    U.S. (Onondaga Indian)

The Turtle Who Couldn't Stop Talking 49
    India

The Story of Arachne 51
    Greece

Rabbit Counts the Crocodiles 54
    Japan

The Straw, the Coal, and the Bean 57
    Germany

How Brazilian Beetles Got Their Gorgeous Coats 59
    Brazil

The Quarrel 62
    U.S. (Cherokee Indian)

Why Parrots Only Repeat What People Say 64
    Thailand

The Taxi Ride 67
    Northern Ghana/Mauritania

How Owl Got His Feathers 69
    Puerto Rico

Two Brothers, Two Rewards 71
    China/Korea/Japan

Why Bear Has a Stumpy Tail 74
    Norway

Where All Stories Come From 76
    U.S. (Seneca Indian)

General Tips for Telling Stories 79

Activities 87

Appendix: Story Sources .91

Introduction

People have always asked "How?" and "Why?" and the answers to these questions have made for some very interesting stories. This book includes a sampling of these kinds of tales, which exist in almost every culture around the world.

Some are known as "pourquoi" stories. *Pourquoi* is the French word for *why*. Pourquoi stories explain why an animal, plant, or natural object looks or acts the way it does. The world is filled with things to wonder about, but we're often in such a rush that we don't notice. Did you ever look carefully, for example, at spiders' webs? If their purpose is simply to catch flies, why do the makers weave such beautiful, intricate things? The ancient Greeks answered that question with the story of Arachne.

Did you ever wonder what causes thunder? Through the ages people around the world have told many different stories to explain the mystery of lightning and thunder. Some said thunder was caused by angels bowling in the sky. Others believed the noise was rocks falling off a wagon or giants fighting. Many Native American peoples tell of an enormous thunderbird whose flapping wings cause lightning and whose voice is thunder. We have included a Nigerian story with a very clever explanation for both thunder and lightning.

Or did you ever take a drive in the country and wonder why, when a car comes down the road, a dog will chase it, a goat will run away, and a donkey will stand right in the middle of the road and not budge? The people of Mauritania and northern Ghana have a story we call "The Taxi Ride" that clears up that question.

Many pourquoi stories certainly must have been made up because a child asked a question like, "Why is the sea salty?" People throughout the world have always enjoyed whimsical answers. Even after we learn the scientific answer to such a question, the stories still appeal to us because they speak to a different side of our brains.

There also are fascinating religious stories or sacred myths that answer big questions such as "How did the world come to be?" "Where did the first people come from?" or "How were the moon and stars formed?" These stories are very important because they help us to find meaning in the world and give purpose and spiritual strength. Because people around the world have different values, it is sometimes difficult to decide whether a tale is a sacred myth or a pourquoi story. Although we have included a few stories that might fall under the category of sacred myth, our focus is on the more amusing pourquoi stories that are told for entertainment.

The tales in this book are fun to read to yourself or out loud to someone else, and they are especially fun to tell! In case you're interested, we've included tips for learning and telling each story *without* the book. Remember, there are many ways to tell a tale: our "tips" are merely suggestions. Your way of telling the story may be completely different, but it will work just as well or even better! We've also included a chapter with general storytelling tips at the end of the book. And because hearing or reading these stories often gives kids (and adults) great ideas for making up and telling their *own* stories, we've offered suggested story titles and activities as well.

Our job for the last twenty years has been telling stories and teaching kids and adults to tell stories. We've found that kids (and adults) are usually nervous and a bit hesitant to tell their first tale. But once they get started, there's often no stopping them. They want to tell again and again in front of other groups. Telling a story is scary at first, but it's a great feeling to see the delight in the eyes of your listeners, and to hear them applaud afterward. So no matter what your age, go on. Take a chance. First, read these stories and then try telling one, or two, or three, or all of them! The rewards are well worth it. As one eight-year-old storyteller wrote after telling her story to a large group of classmates and parents, "I was afraid that my heart would just pound when I got up and looked at all those people. But I learned I'm not as shy as I thought. I felt famous when everyone clapped for me. I felt so good I thought I could fly. And the really good thing I learned about storytelling is you can do it any time, any place."

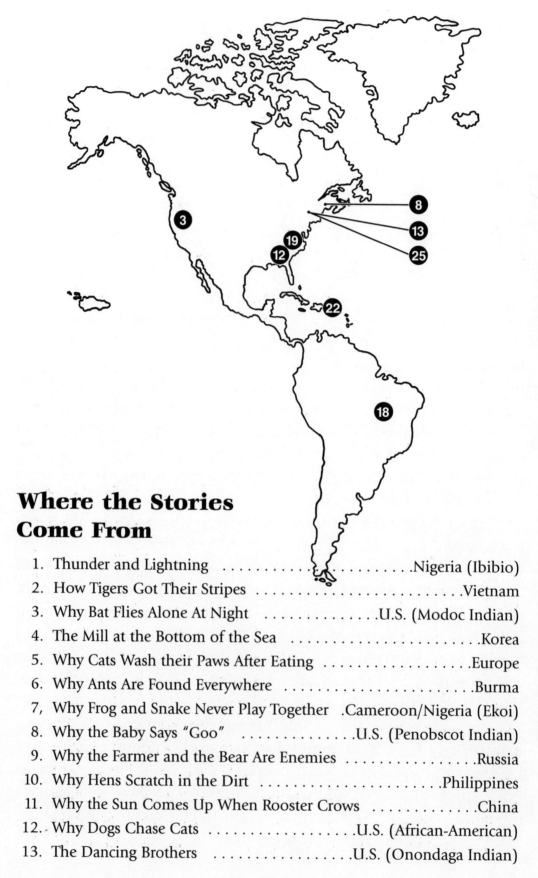

Where the Stories
Come From

1. Thunder and Lightning .Nigeria (Ibibio)
2. How Tigers Got Their Stripes . . . . .Vietnam
3. Why Bat Flies Alone At Night . . . . .U.S. (Modoc Indian)
4. The Mill at the Bottom of the Sea . . . . .Korea
5. Why Cats Wash their Paws After Eating . . . . .Europe
6. Why Ants Are Found Everywhere . . . . .Burma
7. Why Frog and Snake Never Play Together .Cameroon/Nigeria (Ekoi)
8. Why the Baby Says "Goo" . . . . .U.S. (Penobscot Indian)
9. Why the Farmer and the Bear Are Enemies . . . . .Russia
10. Why Hens Scratch in the Dirt . . . . .Philippines
11. Why the Sun Comes Up When Rooster Crows . . . . .China
12. Why Dogs Chase Cats . . . . .U.S. (African-American)
13. The Dancing Brothers . . . . .U.S. (Onondaga Indian)

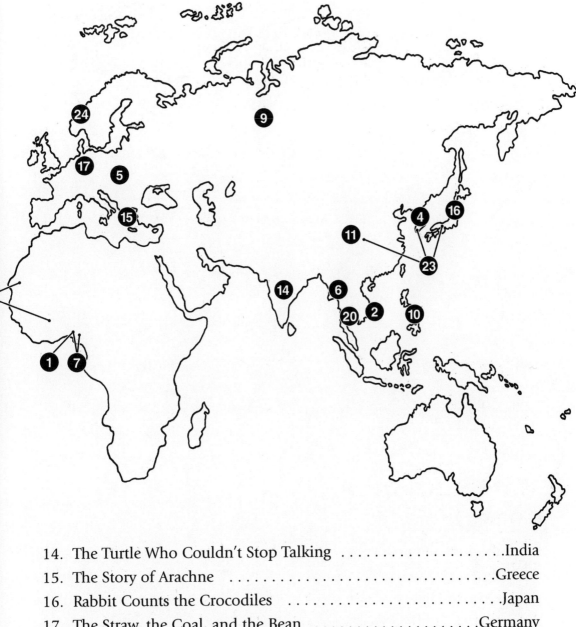

14. The Turtle Who Couldn't Stop Talking . . . . .India

15. The Story of Arachne . . . . .Greece

16. Rabbit Counts the Crocodiles . . . . .Japan

17. The Straw, the Coal, and the Bean . . . . .Germany

18. How Brazilian Beetles Got Their Gorgeous Coats . . . . .Brazil

19. The Quarrel . . . . .U.S. (Cherokee Indian)

20. Why Parrots Only Repeat What People Say . . . . .Thailand

21. The Taxi Ride .Northern Ghana/Mauritania

22. How Owl Got His Feathers . . . . .Puerto Rico

23. Two Brothers, Two Rewards . . . . .China/Korea/Japan

24. Why Bear Has a Stumpy Tail . . . . .Norway

25. Where All Stories Come From . . . . .U.S. (Seneca Indian)

Thunder and Lightning

A Story from the Ibibio* People of Southern Nigeria

Long ago, Lightning and Thunder lived in a small village right here on the earth. Thunder was a mother sheep. Her son, Lightning, was a young ram who had a very bad temper. When he got angry he tore through the countryside burning houses and knocking down large trees. He would scorch the farmers' fields with his fire, and he killed anyone who got in his way.

When his mother, Thunder, saw that he was misbehaving, she would yell at him to stop. Her booming voice was so loud that it shook the houses in the village. The people held their ears. Babies cried. Dogs howled.

Thunder's deafening yells might have been worth it if they had made Lightning stop. But her scolding only made him angrier, so he would start even more fires. And his mother would then yell even louder.

When the people couldn't stand it any longer, they complained to the king. After listening to the villagers, the king forced Thunder and Lightning to live in the bush** far away from everyone else.

But this did not solve the problem. Lightning still couldn't control his terrible temper. He set the trees in the bush

* Ibibio is pronounced *ee-BEE-bee-oh.*

** The *bush* is a thickly wooded wild area.

on fire. The flames soon spread to the farmers' crops. And even though they were further away, Thunder's earsplitting cries still sounded almost as loud as ever.

The villagers once again complained to the king. He was so angry that he banished Thunder and Lightning from the earth. He sent them to live in the sky where the young ram's fire would not hurt the people, and his mother's cries would not be heard.

At first it seemed as if this punishment had worked. But then one day, there was a storm like no one had ever seen before. Great streaks of lightning struck the earth and set things on fire. And after each burst of light, there was a loud booming sound. People soon realized that it was the young ram and his mother up to their old tricks.

And so it is to this very day. Whenever there's a thunderstorm, it's because Lightning has grown angry and thrown his bolts down to the earth. Not long after that, you'll hear his mother, Thunder, angrily scolding him with her booming voice.

About the story

Lightning is a massive surge of electricity in a cloud. It can travel within one cloud, from one cloud to another, or down to the ground. A lightning flash carries an electrical charge that is a million times greater than the charge running through the wires in our homes. Lightning strikes cause more than ten thousand forest fires in the United States each year. Thunder is the sound wave produced when the hot air along a lightning bolt expands and explodes.

If you are interested in reading more world stories that explain thunder and lightning, see if your local library owns *Tales of Thunder and Lightning*, by Harry Devlin (NY: Parents' Magazine Press, 1973).

Tips for telling

When telling this story you must convey with your voice, face, and body just how hard it is for the villagers to live with Thunder and Lightning. When you say, "He tore through the countryside burning houses and knocking down large trees," use hand motions that suggest tearing and knocking down. When you describe how Thunder's voice hurt the ears of the villagers, you may want to hold your hands up to your ears and have a pained look on your face.

You will want to be especially dramatic at the end when you describe the storm. For example, when you say, "After each burst of light there was a loud booming sound," you could emphasize the words *burst* and *booming* and make an appropriate hand gesture at the same time.

How Tigers Got Their Stripes

A Story from Vietnam

Long ago, the tiger had a magnificent golden coat, of which he was very proud. Although we may think the striped coat the tiger has today is beautiful, the tiger hates his stripes. This is the story of how he came to have them.

One morning, as the tiger lay on a hillside, he noticed a water buffalo pulling a plow for his master in the field below. The tiger wondered why a huge beast would do whatever the farmer told him to. He had to find out.

As soon as the farmer went home for lunch, the tiger bounded down to the field.

The water buffalo saw him coming and got into a fighting position. But the tiger said, "Relax, friend. I've come to ask you a question, not to fight with you. I'm very puzzled. You're much bigger than the farmer and could easily defeat him. Why do you work for him?"

"Well," replied the water buffalo, "in return for my work, the farmer takes care of me. I have a barn to live in and plenty of food. But even if he treated me badly, I couldn't escape. You see, he does have some sort of magic that allows him to rule over all his animals. It's called wisdom."

"What's wisdom?" asked the tiger.

"I don't know what it is," said the water buffalo, "but I've heard it's very hard to defeat someone who has it."

"I must find out about this wisdom," said the tiger. "I'm already one of the strongest animals on earth. If I had wisdom, no one could defeat me."

As soon as the farmer returned from lunch, the tiger rushed over to him and said, "Farmer, I've been told that you have something called wisdom. I would like to get some for myself."

Although the farmer was terrified, he thought quickly and replied, "Why, Tiger, I wish you had told me this before I went home for lunch. You see, I've left my wisdom at home. But I'll be glad to go back and get it and share my wisdom with you."

The farmer turned to leave, but after he had taken a few steps, he turned back and said, "It's not that I don't trust you, Tiger. But I am a little worried that you might get hungry and eat my water buffalo. Since I'm willing to share my wisdom with you, would you let me tie you to a tree while I'm gone?"

The foolish tiger was so overcome by his desire to have wisdom that he agreed. The farmer told the tiger to stand upright against a tree. He wound a thick rope many times around the tiger until he was tightly bound. Then the farmer went back to his plowing.

The tiger cried, "What are you doing, Farmer? You promised to go get your wisdom!"

The farmer paid no attention. He kept plowing all afternoon while the tiger kicked and screamed and tried to break free of the rope. Just before the sun went down, the farmer turned to leave. The tiger wailed in anger, but the farmer left without saying a word.

All through the night the tiger tried to break free from the ropes. The more he struggled, the more he felt the ropes burn into his skin. At last, with a great show of strength, the tiger burst free. But his beautiful golden coat was changed forever. He now had black stripes where the ropes had bound him. And to this day, the tiger hates those stripes. They remind him that he *still* doesn't have wisdom.

About the story

A tiger's stripes help it blend in with the tall grasses where it hides to stalk prey. Because deer and other animals it preys upon see mostly in black and white, they don't notice the tiger's orange coloring at all.

Now and then, kids have asked us a question such as, "We understand how this one tiger got stripes, but why is it then true for *all* tigers?" That's a good question. Our usual answer is something like, "That's the way the story goes." Maybe you can come up with a better one...

Tips for telling

When telling this story you will want to convince the audience of the tiger's power. Hold yourself up straight and make your voice deeper when the tiger speaks. The water buffalo also needs to have a deep voice. Because he is a slow, plodding kind of animal, perhaps you could speak more slowly and slump your shoulders a bit for him. Practice while looking in the mirror or have a friend watch and give you tips.

Be sure to use your arms and upper body to show how the tiger struggles to get free from the rope. When the tiger finally bursts free, make a suitable gesture with your hands.

Why Bat Flies
Alone At Night

A Story of the Modoc* Indians

Long ago, the birds and the animals were at war. They fought many battles. During one battle, Bat fought on the birds' side. But things didn't go well for the birds that day. When Bat realized the birds might lose, he flew up into a tree and hung upside down.

When the fighting was over and the animals had won, Bat decided to go home with them. Lion noticed this and said, "Bat, why are you coming with us? You were fighting against us!"

"Oh, no," said Bat. "I wouldn't do that. I'm one of you. I'm an animal. Look at my teeth. None of the birds have teeth."

The animals agreed that this was true, so they let Bat go with them. Not long after that, there was another battle. When the birds started to win, Bat hid under a log and waited till the fighting was over. As the birds flew home, Bat went right along with them.

"Wait a second," said Eagle. "You're one of our enemies! I saw you fighting on the animals' side."

"Oh, no," said Bat. "You're wrong. I'm not an animal. Just look at my wings. Have you ever seen an animal with wings?"

The birds had to admit that this was true, so they let Bat go home with them.

As long as the war lasted, Bat went home with the winning side each day.

* Modoc is pronounced *MO-dock*. These Native Americans battled the U.S. Army in the 1870s to maintain their homelands in northern California and southern Oregon. Despite their overwhelming defeat, there are several hundred descendents living today.

By the end of the war, the animals and birds were furious with Bat. They got together and held a big council to decide what to do. At last they said, "Bat, you lied to us. We don't want to see you again. From now on, you will fly only at night."

To this day, the birds and animals have not forgiven Bat. He still flies alone at night.

About the story

Hundreds of species of bats are found all over the world. Because they are such curious creatures, there are many stories explaining their appearance and behavior. Bats, even though they have wings, are not considered to be birds. In every other way they are like mammals. For example, they have teeth, fur, and a four-chambered heart.

Bats are able to fly at night because they "hear" rather than "see" their way around. They make sounds that are much too high for humans to hear. These sounds travel through the night sky until they strike an object such as a flying insect. The sounds then bounce back and bats hear them with their huge ears. In this way bats know where they're going, even in the middle of the darkest night.

If you'd like to read more about bats, check your library for *Bats: Shadows in the Night,* by Diane Ackerman (NY: Crown, 1997) and *Bats: Swift Shadows in the Twilight,* by Ann C. Cooper (Niwot, CO: Roberts Rinehart Publishers, 1994).

Tips for telling

Speak in an angry voice when Lion and Eagle ask Bat why he's coming with them. Look right at your listeners and pretend they are Bat as you speak. When Bat responds, pretend to be very innocent. You might want to point to your teeth, and later to your imaginary wings, as you speak for Bat.

As in most stories, the last sentence here is very important because it ties the story together. Be sure to say every word clearly. Don't rush!

The Mill at the Bottom of the Sea

A Story from Korea

Long ago, there lived a king who had a very unusual grinding mill. It looked like any other hand mill, but it had special powers. If you wanted something, all you had to do was tell the mill, crank its handle, and you'd get just what you wanted. If you asked for gold, gold would come out. If you asked for rice, rice would come out. Whatever you wanted, the mill would give it to you.

A thief made up his mind to steal the mill. First, he came up with a plan to find out where the king kept it. He dressed like a wealthy man and visited with one of the king's counselors. They chatted about this and that, and finally the thief said, "I heard that the king buried his mill in the ground because he doesn't trust his counselors."

"Where did you hear such talk?" asked the official. "The king trusts me and his other counselors completely!"

"That's what I heard from the people in the countryside," said the thief, happy he had sparked the man's anger. "They say the king dug a deep hole and buried the mill because he is so afraid that someone will steal it."

"That's nonsense!" said the counselor. "The king's mill is beside the lotus pond in the inner court."

"Oh, really?" said the thief, trying to control his excitement.

"No one would dare try to steal the king's hand mill," said the counselor, "especially since it's sitting where there

are always lots of people coming and going."

The thief was so excited that all he could say was "Yes" and "That's right" until he was able to leave.

For many days he watched and waited. Then one very dark night, he climbed the palace wall and stole the hand mill. But when he got outside the palace, he was overcome with fear. He knew that everyone in the city and on the roads would be questioned once the king realized the mill was gone. He decided to steal a boat and go to his hometown to hide.

Once at sea, the thief was able to relax. He began to sing and dance as he thought about how rich he was going to be. Then he thought about what to request from the hand mill. He decided not to ask for gold because people would be suspicious if he suddenly became wealthy.

"I've got it! I'll ask for salt! Everyone needs salt. I can sell it and become a rich man. I'll be the richest man in the country."

He fell down on his knees and began turning the hand mill, demanding, "Salt! Make me some salt!" And sure enough, salt began to pour out of the mill. The thief danced about the boat, thinking about the big house and many servants he would soon have.

However, he didn't realize that the hand mill was still turning and turning. Salt spilled over the sides of the small boat. Finally, the boat was so full of salt that it sank to the bottom of the sea. And, since no one has ever told the hand mill to stop, it's still turning and making salt, which is why the sea is salty.

About the story

Many cultures have stories that explain why the sea is salty, and all of them seem to involve a mill that lies at the bottom. One well-known version comes from Scandinavia.

Why *is* the sea salty? As rivers flow down the mountains and over the land, they tear loose minerals, most of which are different kinds of salts. Although there's never enough salt in a river to make the water taste salty, rivers have been dumping tons of salt into the oceans for millions of years, so the sea is *very* salty.

Tips for telling

When you describe the mill at the beginning of the story, make it sound very unusual. When you say, "Gold would come out," you could make a hand gesture as if to show it flowing out. At the same time, pretend to watch in amazement as you see the gold.

The king's counselor should sound very insulted and angry when the thief tells him the king is hiding the mill. When the thief discovers the location of the mill, show that he's very excited but trying to control his emotions so the counselor won't suspect anything.

When the thief climbs over the palace wall, speak softly and look all around as if you don't want to be discovered. Sound frightened when the thief realizes that the king's men will look everywhere for the mill. Your expression should turn to joy once he makes his escape and plans his great fortune. Pretend to crank the mill's handle and greedily ask for salt. Use hand motions to show the salt filling up the boat and spilling over the sides. As you say, "the boat sank to the bottom of the sea," make a downward motion with your hand.

Why Cats Wash Their Paws After Eating

A Story from Europe

Cat was hungry. She spied a bird and thought, "There's my dinner!" She crept toward it slowly and quietly, and kept very close to the ground. Then she pounced on the bird and grabbed it between her paws.

Just as she was about to take a big bite, Bird said, "Cat, I'm surprised at you! I have *never* met a cat with such bad manners. Don't you wash your paws before you eat?"

Cat didn't want anyone, not even a bird, to think she had bad manners. So she began to lick her paws and clean herself. Of course, Bird quickly flew to a nearby tree.

Since that time, Cat eats first and *then* washes her paws.

About the story

All cats hunt. When they find a good hunting spot, they sit and wait. When their prey appears, they pounce. Even indoor cats will find something to hunt. They will "capture" a ball (or any toy) and "kill" it just like real prey.

Cats spend a great deal of time grooming themselves. They do this in a particular order. They start by licking their lips and then wetting the sides of their paws. Then they begin with their faces and clean all the way down to the tips of their tails. When they're finished, they stretch and preen, almost as if to say, "Look at me! Look how clean and beautiful I am!"

Tips for telling

When you say, "She spied a bird," pretend to see a bird in front of you. Look excited and hungry as you say, "There's my dinner!" Then, while standing in one place, pretend to creep toward the bird as if you're sneaking up on it. Both *pounced* and *grabbed* are great action words, so you may want to make a hand gesture as you say them. When you pretend to speak for the bird, be sure to act really shocked at the cat's behavior. You could put your hands on your hips and have a look of disgust on your face as you say, "Cat, I'm surprised at you!"

Why Ants are Found Everywhere

A Story from Burma*

One day, Lion, the king of the beasts, ordered all the other animals to honor him. One by one, Tiger, Elephant, Snake, Lizard, and many other animals came to bow before Lion.

Even Ant set out on the long journey. It was not an easy trip for him. Whenever he came to a rock or vine, he had to crawl up one side and down the other. As a result, Ant was the last to arrive. When the animals saw Ant coming, they made fun of him. Lion roared with laughter and said, "It's about time you got here!"

Ant crawled away in shame. He told the Queen of the Ants how badly Lion had treated him. The Ant Queen was furious. She asked her friend Worm to crawl in Lion's ear and torture him.

Worm crept into Lion's ear. He twisted and turned. He wiggled and jiggled. Lion roared. He shook his head back and forth trying to get Worm out. The other animals offered to help, but none was small enough. Lion knew he would go crazy if he didn't find a way to get rid of Worm.

At last he realized there was only one animal that could help him. Lion sent a messenger to the Ant Queen. He asked her to send someone to crawl

*Burma, a country in southeastern Asia, also is known as Myanmar (pronounced *MYUN-mar*).

in his ear and get Worm out. The Ant Queen decided Lion had been punished enough, so she sent Ant to help.

When Ant finally arrived, Lion was rolling on the ground in pain. Ant crawled into his ear and called out, "Thank you, Worm. You can come out now."

Lion was so relieved that he rewarded Ant. He said, "Well done, Ant. I have decided that from now on you and your people may live anywhere you'd like."

And that is why, to this day, even though some animals can live only in the jungle, some only in the desert, and others only in the rain forest, ants live *everywhere*.

About the story

Ants really do live everywhere. They are found from the Arctic to the tropics, in deserts, forests, fields, cities, mountains, and beaches. For this reason, they play a large part in the folktales of the world.

Tips for telling

You may want to pretend to bow when you say, "Many other animals came to bow before him." Use a hand motion when you describe how Ant had to crawl "up one side and down the other." Be sure to use motions for Worm twisting and turning in Lion's ear and for Lion shaking his head back and forth. Say, "Lion was rolling on the ground in pain" with great feeling so that listeners can see the picture in their minds.

When you say "everywhere" at the very end of the story, make a circular gesture with both hands, one to the left, the other to the right.

Why Frog and Snake
Never Play Together

A Story told by the Ekoi* People of Cameroon and Nigeria

One day, a small frog went out to play. While hopping through the forest, he met a creature he had never seen before. It was long and thin and had a coat of many different colors.

"Who are you?" asked Frog.

"I'm a snake. Who are you?"

"I'm a frog. Would you like to play together?"

"Sure," hissed Snake.

So Snake and Frog spent a great morning in the forest. Frog taught his new friend how to hop. It took a lot of practice, but soon Snake was hopping almost as well as a frog. He couldn't wait to show his family!

In return, Snake taught Frog how to crawl on his belly. Frog thought it was the best thing he had ever done. Now he'd be able to sneak up on his friends and then jump up and scare them.

When it was time to go home for lunch, Frog said, "You're the best friend I ever had!"

"That was so much fun," agreed Snake. "See you tomorrow."

They hugged each other and then rushed home. Frog said, "Mother, watch what I can do!" And he got down on his belly and slithered across the floor.

Mother Frog was suspicious. "Where did you learn to do *that?*"

"My new friend Snake taught me," Frog answered proudly.

* Ekoi is pronounced *EH-koy.*

Mother Frog's mouth fell wide open. "Did you say snake?" she asked. "That's right, he's my new best friend."

"Are you crazy? Don't you know that snakes eat frogs? Frogs are not *friends* for snakes. Frogs are *food* for snakes. Our families have always been enemies. You must never play with him again!"

"Oh, mother, my new friend would never eat me," said Frog.

"Oh, yes he will," warned his mother. "He's a snake. That's what snakes do to us frogs. You stay away from him. And cut out that slithery stuff. Frogs don't do that. I'll have none of that in my house!"

Frog wondered about what his mother had said. He remembered that Snake had hugged him a little too hard.

Meanwhile, when Snake returned home to his family, he said, "I bet you can't do this." And he jumped high into the air. His brothers and sisters laughed, but his mother was horrified.

"Who taught you to do such a foolish thing?" she demanded.

"It was my new friend Frog. He's great. Wait till you see *him* jump!"

His mother screeched, "Listen here! Snakes don't jump. You cut that out right now! And snakes don't play with frogs. They eat them. Frogs are not *friends* for snakes. Frogs are *food* for snakes. Next time you see Frog, you grab him and eat him!"

Snake didn't know what to say. "I'd never do that to my good friend."

"Oh, yes you will," said his mother. "Snakes have been catching and eating frogs since the beginning of time. It's what we snakes do."

Snake wondered about what his mother had said. When they had hugged, it had felt *really* good to squeeze Frog.

The next morning Snake slithered over to Frog's house and called, "Come on out and play."

Frog didn't even open the door. He yelled, "Thanks, but I have other plans today. In fact, I can't play with you *ever* again."

"Oh, I see that your mother has talked to you. Well, my mother has talked to me, too. I guess that's the end of our friendship." Then Snake slithered home sadly.

Frog and Snake have never played together since. But to this day, both snakes and frogs often sit quietly in the sun. When they do, they're wondering what would have happened if they had never told their mothers. They might still be playing together.

About the story
A wonderful version of this story may be found in Ashley Bryan's book *Beat the Story-Drum, Pum-Pum* (NY: Macmillan, 1980). His version is quite long, but it's beautifully written and well worth reading. It may give you other ideas you'd like to incorporate into your telling of the story.

Tips for telling
This is a really fun story to tell. You'll want to show the feeling of Snake and Frog having a great time. Use hand gestures for hopping and slithering. Show great anger when you speak as the mothers. When you speak as Snake or his mother, you may want to draw out your *s* sounds.

Why the Baby Says "Goo"

A Story of the Penobscot*
Indians of Maine

Gluscabe** was a trickster and a great hero of the Penobscot people. He wasn't afraid of anything. He led the warriors in battle, drove off the ice giants from the north, and defeated the spirits that lived in the mountains.

Wherever Gluscabe went, people praised him for his great deeds. Because of this, Gluscabe began to grow vain. He walked about boasting, "I can conquer anyone!"

A wise old woman heard him and said, "Although you have great courage, there's one you have never conquered, and never will."

"Grandmother, why do you doubt me?" replied Gluscabe. "Who is this mighty warrior?"

"Why, he happens to be in my wigwam right now," said the old woman. She then pulled back the flap of her little hut. A baby sat in the middle of the floor, cooing and sucking on a piece of maple sugar.

Gluscabe had no wife and knew nothing about babies. He burst out laughing and said, "Old woman, have you lost your mind? There's nothing but a baby in your wigwam. He'll surely obey me."

Then Gluscabe said, "Baby, come to me." Much to his surprise, the baby smiled and kept on sucking his maple sugar. Gluscabe was confused. The people always did what he told them. Maybe the baby hadn't heard him. So he called out again, "Baby, come to me!"

*Penobscot is pronounced *pen-AHB-scot.*

**Gluscabe is pronounced *GLOOS-kah-bee*

Again the little baby smiled, but Gluscabe was not amused. He was angry. This time he yelled, "BABY, COME TO ME!"

But the little baby didn't go to Gluscabe. Instead, he burst out crying and screaming. Gluscabe held his hands over his ears and said to the old woman, "Oh! This baby's war cries are the loudest I've ever heard. Even the cries of the ice giants aren't this bad! Maybe I can stop this little warrior with some magic."

Then Gluscabe took out his medicine bag and shook it at the baby. The baby soon stopped wailing. But when Gluscabe put it away, the baby started to cry once again.

Gluscabe tried dancing. The baby loved that! But when Gluscabe stopped and said, "Come to me," the baby wailed again. So Gluscabe danced again. The baby clapped his hands and laughed. Sweat began to run down Gluscabe's face. He danced on and on until he was too tired to dance anymore. He sat down with a look of defeat on his face.

The old woman said, "Don't be discouraged. No one is mightier than the baby. He always rules the wigwam. Everyone loves and obeys him. No one wants to hear that awful crying."

Gluscabe didn't reply. He just gave a big sigh and turned to leave. He looked at the baby, who sat on the floor happily saying, "Goo, goo."

To this day, babies often sit happily saying, "goo, goo!" for no obvious reason. Now you know why. It's because they still remember the time the baby proved he was mightier than Gluscabe.

About the story

Anyone who has ever spent much time around a baby knows the truth in this story. The theme is found in tales from many cultures. In one Romanian story, a decision must be made about who is the greatest in the land. In the end, the baby is judged to be far stronger even than a king or a prince because no one can control it.

Tips for telling

Hold your body tall and straight with shoulders high for Gluscabe. You may want to bend over a bit, as if leaning on a cane, when you pretend to be the old woman. When Gluscabe dances, move your arms as if to dance. Do just enough so that the listeners can see Gluscabe dancing in their minds. If you get carried away and really dance, your listeners will see only *you* and not use their imaginations. You don't want to get in the way of the story.

Why the Farmer and the Bear are Enemies

A Story from Russia

One beautiful spring day, a farmer was plowing his ground to plant carrots, when a bear wandered by. The bear was just about to grab him, but the farmer begged, "Don't hurt me, Bear. Why don't we farm together? I'll do all the work for both of us. You can have everything that grows *above* the ground, and I'll take the roots."

"That sounds fair," said the bear. "But you'd better not try to trick me, or you won't be safe in the woods anymore!"

The carrots the farmer planted grew to be quite large. At last the day came to harvest them. When they were all dug up, the farmer said to the bear, "Now let's divide them evenly. Just as I promised, you get all the tops, and I get the roots."

The bear was quite pleased with the huge bundle of carrot leaves he took home. But he was not pleased with their bitter taste. He returned to the farmer and demanded to taste one of the roots. The bear ate a carrot and said, "These are sweet and delicious. You've tricked me, Farmer. You had better not go in the woods again!"

"I'm sorry, Bear. I didn't mean to trick you. Next year you can have all the roots, and I'll take what grows above the ground. It's only fair."

But the next year, the farmer didn't plant carrots. Instead, he planted wheat. He figured since he was doing all the work, he should get the best end of the deal. When it was time to harvest the wheat, the bear showed up again. The farmer gave the bear all the roots and then loaded the wheat in his wagon.

When the bear got home, he couldn't think of anything to do with the roots. He was furious! He went to the farmer's house and warned him, "You've shown how smart you are, Farmer. But if you're really smart, from now on you'll stay out of my woods!"

To this day, the farmer is always a little nervous when he goes into the woods. And with good reason, for the bear still hasn't forgiven the farmer for tricking him.

About the story

The theme of one person or animal tricking another by dividing crops unevenly appears in the folklore of many countries. We found African-American, Japanese, Dutch, Serbian, French, and Scandinavian versions, just to mention a few. The crops are different, but the idea is the same.

Tips for telling

Hold your shoulders high and use a deep voice for the bear. When the farmer and bear first meet, you could pretend to reach for the farmer to grab him. The bear must grow angrier each time the farmer tricks him. At the end, be sure to have a worried expression as you explain that the farmer is always a "little nervous" when he goes into the woods.

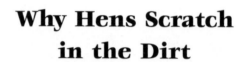

Why Hens Scratch
in the Dirt

A Story from the Philippines

Although the hen and the hawk are bitter enemies today, this wasn't always so. In fact, long ago the hawk asked the hen to marry him. She was quite fond of him, so she agreed. The next day, the hawk bought a ring and gave it to her.

Not long afterward, the rooster came to court the hen. He saw the ring she was wearing and asked, "Where did you get that ring?"

The hen replied, "Why, the hawk gave it to me. We're engaged to be married, you know."

The rooster burst out laughing and said, "Well, if he really loved you, he would have gotten you a nicer ring. He probably found that ugly thing lying around on the ground."

The hen had thought the ring was beautiful when the hawk gave it to her. But as she looked at it more carefully, she thought what the rooster said might be true.

"Listen," said the rooster, "why don't you throw that ring away and marry me instead? The hawk doesn't treat you well. We'd make a much better pair."

The rooster went on and on until he convinced the hen that the hawk was not a good match for her. She took the ring off and threw it away. She decided she'd make up some story to tell the hawk.

But a small bird had been listening to their conversation. He flew away to tell the hawk what he had heard.

The next day, when the hawk visited the hen, he asked, "Why aren't you wearing the ring I gave you?"

"I - uh - uh - I lost it," replied the hen.

"You lost it? How on earth did you lose it?" asked the hawk.

"It - uh - it just fell off. I was - uh - I was running away from a lizard, and when I finally stopped to catch my breath - it - uh - the ring was - uh - gone."

"You're lying to me," said the hawk.

"Oh no, I wouldn't lie to you."

"Yes, you would! You've made up the whole story. I know you threw my ring away so you could get engaged to that know-it-all rooster."

The hen hung her head when she realized the hawk had caught her in a lie.

"It's true that I couldn't afford an expensive ring," said the hawk. "But I was always true to you. Now I don't want anything to do with you, for you were not a true friend to me."

The hen didn't say anything. She just kept looking at the ground.

The hawk said, "I want my ring back. You had better start looking for it. Until you find it, I will come whenever I'm hungry and help myself to your chicks."

The hen felt so bad about what she'd done that she set out to look for the ring right away. She scratched and scratched in the dirt, looking everywhere.

But to this day, she hasn't found it. When you see a bunch of hens, they're always scratching in the dirt, still looking for that ring. And the hawks are still stealing chickens as payment.

About the story

Hens really scratch in the dirt because they're looking for worms and bugs to eat, but this makes for a more interesting story.

The name *hawk* comes from a word meaning "to seize or take hold"—a reference to the way in which these birds grasp their prey. Many farmers call all hawks "chicken hawks," even though the majority of hawks are more useful to them than harmful. Hawks sometimes do eat chicks, but they usually eat rabbits, rodents, and insects, all of which are troublesome to farmers.

Tips for telling

When the hen is speaking to either the rooster or the hawk, turn slightly from one side to the other as the conversation goes back and forth. Practice this in the mirror to make sure it really looks as if two speakers are talking to one another. Don't turn too much to the side or your voice will go there rather than out to your listeners. It should be as if you're turning to look first toward the left side of the audience and then to the right.

The hen should appear to be very nervous when she is lying to the hawk about the ring. The hawk should respond angrily to her.

Why the Sun Comes Up
When Rooster Crows

A Story from China

Long ago, when the world was young, there wasn't just one sun in the sky. There were nine. Their blazing heat scorched the land. The earth grew hotter and hotter. The crops shriveled. People began to die.

The people tried to think of ways to block the heat of the nine suns. Finally, they decided to ask their best archer to shoot the suns out of the sky. He listened to their plan and agreed to help.

The next morning before sunrise, the archer climbed to the top of the highest mountain. As each sun appeared, he strung an arrow and, one by one, shot the suns. He did this eight times until there was only one sun left. As the last sun watched what happened to her sisters, she grew more and more terrified. She hid behind a mountain so that she would not be pierced by an arrow.

At first the people celebrated their victory. They praised the archer for his great skill. But they soon realized that they couldn't live without the sun. The world was now freezing cold. Nothing would grow. They called out to the hiding sun, but no matter what they said, she wouldn't come out.

A great meeting was called to decide what to do. "We must find someone who can convince the sun that we mean no harm."

A few people suggested Tiger. They said, "Tiger is a powerful animal. His words will be believed by the sun."

But Tiger's voice was so loud and sounded so much like a growl that the sun grew even more frightened.

One of the village elders spoke up. "Perhaps we need an animal that has a soothing voice. Why not ask Oriole? No one sings better than Oriole."

Oriole sang her sweetest song. Although the sun liked Oriole's singing, she still wouldn't come out. Many other birds tried, but none of them succeeded.

At last, another of the elders suggested Rooster. He argued, "It's true that Rooster doesn't sing as beautifully as Oriole, but he's fearless and won't give up." When the people asked Rooster, he didn't hesitate. He strutted to the top of the mountain and called out, "Cock-a-doodle-doo!"

The sun was still too scared to come out. Rooster crowed a second time, "Cock-a-doodle-doo!" A tiny bit of the sun peeked out from behind the mountain. She was still afraid that she would be shot with an arrow. When Rooster crowed a third time, the sun was convinced that it was safe. Her fear vanished, and she came out from behind the mountain in her full glory.

The crowd cheered. The sun was very pleased with their reaction. She was grateful to Rooster for finally convincing her to come out. To reward him, she took a bit of red out of the morning sky, made it into the shape of a comb, and placed it on top of Rooster's head.

To this day, Rooster is very proud that he saved the world. If you watch him in the barnyard, you will see that he struts about with his chest puffed out and the bright red comb on his head. And every morning when Rooster crows, the sun soon appears.

About the story

On any farm, the rooster's crowing is the first sign of morning. His ear-splitting "Cock-a-doodle-doo" reminds everyone that he is number one—the strongest male in the roost. His red comb is so distinctive, it's no wonder people made up stories that explained its creation.

It's also not surprising that every country and culture has many stories to explain various features of the sun. Life as we know it wouldn't be possible without its warm rays. There are parts of the world, however, where the sun's blinding heat makes life almost unbearable. The people who live there sometimes may wish the sun would go away, but if it did, they certainly would regret it, just as the people in this story did.

Tips for telling

At the beginning of the story, make it sound as if the people on earth are in a desperate situation. When the archer shoots the suns out of the sky, pretend to pull back a bow and watch the arrow soar through the air.

Each time Rooster says, "Cock-a-doodle-doo!" puff yourself up and strut a bit. Afterward, show that the sun is growing less and less scared each time Rooster crows. When the sun finally comes out from behind the mountain, you may want to spread your arms to show that she is shining "in her full glory." At the very end, be sure again to show with your body that Rooster thinks he's the greatest.

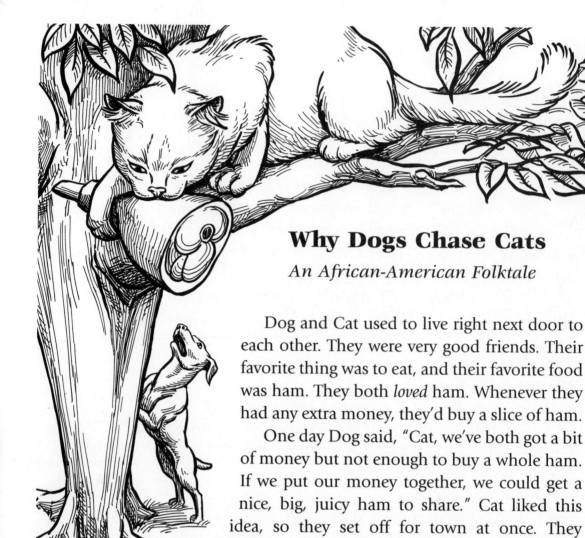

Why Dogs Chase Cats

An African-American Folktale

Dog and Cat used to live right next door to each other. They were very good friends. Their favorite thing was to eat, and their favorite food was ham. They both *loved* ham. Whenever they had any extra money, they'd buy a slice of ham.

One day Dog said, "Cat, we've both got a bit of money but not enough to buy a whole ham. If we put our money together, we could get a nice, big, juicy ham to share." Cat liked this idea, so they set off for town at once. They bought a huge ham. It was so heavy they had to take turns carrying it home.

As Dog carried the meat, he sang, "Our ham, our ham, our ham."

Then it was Cat's turn. When she smelled that delicious ham, she thought, "I sure would like to eat that whole ham *all* by myself." So without thinking, she sang, "My ham, my ham, my ham."

Dog was suspicious about Cat's song, but he didn't say anything. When he carried it again, he sang, "Our ham, our ham, our ham."

As they got near their homes, Cat was carrying the ham, singing, "My ham, my ham, my ham." Suddenly she sprang up a tree and began to gobble down the ham.

Since Dog couldn't climb the tree, all he could do was sit there and watch Cat stuff down the *whole* ham. Dog grew madder and madder. He barked louder and louder. When Cat was finished, she just smacked her lips and rubbed her stomach.

Dog yelled up at her, "Cat, when you get hungry again and come down for *your* supper, I'm gonna eat *you* for *my* supper!"

Cat finally did get hungry. And ever since she came down from the tree, Dog's been chasing her. He still hasn't forgiven her for eating the *whole* ham.

About the story

Although some dogs and cats seem to live together peacefully, most want nothing to do with one another. Many cultures have stories to explain why dogs and cats don't get along. One story told in many Asian countries involves a dog and cat who are sent to deliver a ring. On the way the ring is lost, and to this day, each blames the other.

Tips for telling

When the dog and cat carry the ham, pretend to hold it as you sing. You could carry it on your shoulder or in both arms as you would a baby. Practice with a mirror. Remember, that ham is heavy! You may want to use a bit deeper voice for the dog. Then when the cat sings, have her look longingly at the ham. Show that she just can't control herself. Move your eyebrows up and down and have a very greedy look on your face. The more you get into the story and really sing, the more your listeners will enjoy it.

At the end, pretend to look up at the cat in the tree as you shout angrily at her.

The Dancing Brothers

A Story of the Onondaga Indians*

In a time long ago, there lived eight brothers. Late one fall, their mother and father went to a special ceremony and feast of thanksgiving. The boys begged to go, but they were told the ceremony was only for adults.

The boys were angry. They crept quietly to the spot where the ceremony was held. They watched as the people gathered around a fire and gave thanks to the Great Spirit. There was singing and dancing, and finally, a feast.

The boys hurried back to their lodge. They decided they would have their own ceremony. They went to their favorite spot in the forest and built a fire. The oldest boy began to beat a small drum, and they sang songs. Then they all began to dance slowly with the rhythm of the music. Round and round the fire they danced.

Suddenly a strange old man appeared. He was dressed in white feathers and his hair shone like silver. He warned the boys, "If you do not stop this singing and dancing, great evil will come to you."

The boys obeyed the man and returned to their lodge. But the next night, they again stole away to the forest and began to dance. They went round and round until they grew lightheaded and hungry. Since they had not brought any food for a feast, they just kept on dancing. The oldest boy beat the drum faster, and the boys' feet seemed to grow lighter. Before they realized it, their feet had left the ground and they were rising into the sky.

The oldest brother was the first to notice. He warned the others, "Whatever you do, don't look down for something very strange is happening."

Just then, the mother realized her sons were missing. She called their names, but there was no reply. She ran to the spot where they

* Onondaga is pronounced *on-un-DAH-gah.*

loved to play in the forest and found a fire burning. When she looked up, she saw her children rising higher and higher into the sky. She screamed, "Come back!" Only the youngest of the boys heard his mother's cry and looked down. He lost his balance and fell toward the earth. When he hit the ground, he disappeared. All that his mother found was a small hole where he had landed.

The seven older brothers kept on floating upward. They danced faster and faster until they looked like a ring of fire. As they went higher, they became a cluster of stars that is known as the Pleiades.*

Each day during the winter, the mother returned to the spot where her youngest son had fallen. She wept for all her children. The next spring, a little green shoot sprang up from the hole. As the years passed, it grew into the first pine tree. Because the spirit of the youngest brother longed to be near the others, the tree grew straight up, reaching toward the sky world.

To this day, the pine tree grows tall and straight in the forest while his seven brothers still dance in the winter sky.

About the story

The Onondaga are one of the six tribes of the Iroquois Confederacy whose traditional territory included most of New York State. The symbol of peace and unity among the six tribes is a great white pine tree. The pine is a tall, straight tree reaching heights of one hundred feet. It can live to be six hundred years old.

The Pleiades is a loose cluster of stars that is part of the large constellation Taurus. It is

* Pleiades is pronounced *PLEE-uh-deez.*

usually said to consist of seven stars, although some people see only six, and others see more than seven. Many cultures around the world have told stories to explain this and other constellations. If you would like to read more, check your library for *Star Tales: North American Indian Stories about the Stars*, by Gretchen Will Mayo (NY: Walker, 1987) and *They Dance in the Sky*, by Jean G. Monroe and Ray A. Williamson (Boston: Houghton Mifflin, 1987).

Tips for telling

When the boys spy on their parents, pretend to creep up and see the people gathered around the fire. When you describe the boys dancing around the fire, make a big circle with your hand. You might want to use an old man's voice when the stranger speaks. Hunch over a bit and point your finger at your listeners as if they are the dancing boys. Make an upward movement with your arm as the boys rise into the air.

The mother should sound desperate when she discovers that her sons are missing. As the eight boys rise in the sky, look up and pretend to see them. When the youngest son loses his balance, make a movement with your upper body to suggest this. Remember, use just enough movement to help your listeners see pictures in their minds. At the end, show with your eyes, and perhaps your hands as well, how the pine reaches toward the sky.

The Turtle Who Couldn't Stop Talking

A Story from India

Long, long ago, a turtle lived in a pond with two swans. The turtle loved to talk. She always had something to say, and she liked to hear herself say it.

After they had lived in the pond happily for many years, a dry spell came. There was no rain for weeks and weeks. At last the pond dried up completely. The two swans realized they would have to leave their home and fly to another pond with water. They went to say good-bye to their friend, the turtle. But she begged them, "Don't leave me behind! I too have nothing to eat and no water to live on. I will surely die if I'm left here."

"But you can't fly!" said the swans. "How can we take you with us?"

"Take me with you! Please take me with you!" pleaded the turtle.

The swans felt so sorry for their friend that at last they came up with a plan. They said to the turtle, "We have thought of a way to take you with us. We will each take hold of one end of a long stick. You must hold onto the middle of it with your beak and never let go. You must not talk as long as we are carrying you! If you open your mouth, you'll fall to the ground."

The turtle promised not to say a word. Away the swans flew into the air, carrying the turtle on the stick between them. As they rose above the treetops, the turtle wanted to say, "Goodness, look how high we are!" but she remembered the swans' warning.

Soon they passed over a small town, and a few people looked up and shouted, "Look at the swans carrying a turtle! What a silly sight!"

The turtle thought to herself, "Why don't they mind their own business?" but she remembered not to say anything out loud.

Soon more villagers came to see the sight. They cried, "How strange! A flying turtle! Look, everybody!"

The turtle could stand it no longer. She opened her mouth to call out, "Hush, you foolish people!" But as she did, she let go of the stick and fell to the ground. She landed on her back, and her shell cracked into a thousand pieces.

Turtle's shell has remained that way to this day. Her cracked shell reminds us of what can happen if we talk too much.

About the story

When we watch turtles crawl over rocks they easily could have gone around, we may assume they're not very smart. But turtles actually are quite intelligent. They appear in the folklore of many countries, and in most stories are thought to be very wise. Of course, there are exceptions to every rule: the turtle in this story doesn't seem to be wise at all!

Tips for telling

When the swans are warning the turtle not to talk, look right at the audience. You may want to point with your finger as if you're scolding. When you say, "Goodness, look how high we are!" pretend to be the turtle looking down. Show by the expression in your voice and on your face that the turtle is amazed. When the people say, "Look at the swans carrying a turtle!" look up as if you're peering into the sky and pretend to see them. Have the turtle grow angrier and angrier throughout the story until she finally says, "Hush, you foolish people!"

The Story of Arachne

A Story from Ancient Greece

Arachne* was a simple country girl who had a great talent as a weaver. Each day, she set up her loom outside so that she could be inspired by nature. Her fame spread until people came from miles around to watch her weave. They would often say, "Arachne's work is so beautiful. Why, the goddess Athena** herself must have taught Arachne how to weave." It was true that Arachne had been a student of Athena, the goddess of household arts such as weaving and pottery.

But Arachne refused to admit this. She would proudly say, "No one taught *me* how to weave. The goddess Athena could never weave tapestries as lovely as mine." Her father warned her not to compare herself to the goddess. He knew that nothing made the gods angrier than a human being comparing herself with them. But Arachne paid him no mind.

One day Arachne bragged of her skill to the people who had come to watch her. An old woman stepped forward to praise Arachne's weaving.

"Your work is splendid," said the old woman. "But don't be so bold as to claim that it is better than Athena's."

Arachne just laughed. "Go away, old woman. I have no fear of Athena. If Athena's weavings are so beautiful, then I challenge her to a contest!"

Arachne no sooner had said these bold words than the old woman threw back her cloak and revealed that she was actually Athena in disguise! She said to Arachne, "Come, foolish girl, you shall have your contest!"

The two agreed that their subject would be the gods. Many people gathered to watch as the contest began. For hours their shuttles flew swiftly back and forth. When the contest ended, all the onlookers

* Arachne is pronounced *uh-RACK-nee.*

** Athena is pronounced *uth-EE-nuh.*

51

gazed admiringly at Athena's tapestry. She had woven a picture of the gods in all their glory. It was breathtaking.

Then they turned to look at Arachne's tapestry. It, too, was very beautifully woven. It was alive with color. Every thread was perfect. Athena herself was amazed—until she saw that Arachne's weaving showed the gods as fools.

Athena was beside herself with rage. She took up her shuttle and slashed Arachne's weaving in two. Then she touched Arachne with the shuttle. Arachne began to shrivel. Her hair fell away. Her fingers were changed into little black legs. She grew smaller and smaller until she was scarcely larger than a fly.

Then Athena spoke. "Arachne, your pride has brought you down. But you shall continue to weave. You and your children will be among the greatest spinners and weavers on earth."

And it was true. Arachne became the mother of all spiders. To this day, their webs are some of the most beautiful weavings ever made. But because they are usually in dark corners, few people ever see them.

About the story

Arachne is the Greek word for spider. Spiders belong to the biological class arachnids (pronounced *uh-RACK-nidds*).

In the Greek myths, the gods have great powers. They are immortal, which means they will live forever. However, they often do things that don't seem godlike at all— throwing tantrums or seeking revenge when they feel they have been wronged. As shown in this story, it is considered a great sin for human beings to compare themselves with the gods.

Tips for telling

When telling this story you must show with your body language and speech that both Athena and Arachne are extremely proud. Hold yourself tall and straight when you speak for them. Because their manners are similar, it will be important to show differences between the two, especially during the parts where they talk back and forth. Turn very slightly to one side when you speak as Athena and the other way when talking as Arachne.

You may wish to bend over a bit and use an old woman's voice when Athena first appears. At the end, be sure to use hand motions when you describe how Athena slashes Arachne's weaving and when Arachne begins to shrivel and become a spider.

Rabbit Counts the Crocodiles

A Story from Japan

Long ago, Rabbit had a fine, long, bushy tail like a raccoon's. Back then, just as now, he was always up to one kind of trick or another. It was one of his tricks that caused him to lose his long tail. Let me tell you how it happened.

Rabbit lived on the island of Oki,* just off the coast of Japan. Although he had a good life, Rabbit longed to see what it was like on the mainland. He would spend hours staring across the sea, wishing he knew how to swim.

One day when Crocodile swam near the shore, an idea came to Rabbit. He called out, "Crocodile, do you realize I have *hundreds* of rabbits in my family? It's a shame you have so few crocodiles in yours."

"Who told you that?" snapped Crocodile. "Why, there are hundreds, maybe even thousands, of crocodiles in my family!"

This reaction was just what Rabbit had hoped for. "So far, so good," Rabbit thought to himself. "My plan just might work." Then he said to Crocodile, "Well, if there are so many in your family, how come I only see one of you now and then?"

"That's easy," replied Crocodile. "Because we're usually hidden below the water."

"Well, I won't believe it until I see it. Why don't you call all your crocodile family here so I can count them?"

*Oki is pronounced
OH-kee.

Crocodile was furious. She shouted, "Fine, you little ball of fur, you stay right here. I'll show you just how many crocodiles are in my family." Crocodile then dove under the water and disappeared.

Soon many crocodiles began to appear. Before long, there were hundreds and hundreds of crocodiles swimming toward the island.

Rabbit then said to Crocodile, "I must admit that you have a lot of crocodiles in your family. But I can't count them when they're in a big clump like this. Tell them to get in a long line."

The crocodiles made one long, straight line that stretched all the way to the mainland. Rabbit began to hop across the backs of the crocodiles. As he did, he counted, "One, two, three, four, five..." and on and on until he was almost to the mainland.

When he was just about to step on the last crocodile, he couldn't keep from laughing and shouting, "Oh foolish crocodiles, thanks so much for making a bridge for me!"

When the last crocodile heard this, she opened her jaws wide to eat Rabbit. But all she managed to bite off was Rabbit's tail. That's why, to this day, all rabbits have short tails.

About the story

The first two versions we happened to find of this story were from Japan and Uganda (a country in Africa). These two cultures are so different—and yet these two stories are so similar! We eventually found European, Indonesian, and African-American versions as well. Why do so many similar stories exist throughout the world? Why, for example, are there five hundred versions of Cinderella found in Europe alone?

People have puzzled over this issue for a long time. Sometimes the stories were passed from one country to another when people traveled and traded. Others believe there may have been a common origin of all humans, and the stories derived from this original source. Still others argue that stories come out of human experience, and many of our hopes, dreams, and fears are similar, regardless of where we live in the world.

Tips for telling

Rabbit must be portrayed, from beginning to end, as very sure of himself. When Rabbit says, "So far, so good..." pretend you're sharing a secret with the listeners. You may want to lean toward them a bit and cup one hand over your mouth. Make Crocodile sound very annoyed with Rabbit when she says, "Fine, you little ball of fur..."

When Rabbit sees all the other members of Crocodile's family, look out into the audience as if you're seeing hundreds of crocodiles. When the crocodiles form one long line, make a hand gesture to show how it stretches all the way to the mainland. When Rabbit counts the crocodiles, you may want to point as if you're counting the crocodiles in a straight line in front of you.

At the very end of the story, when the crocodile opens her jaws, put your palms together, one on top of the other. Raise the top one as the crocodile opens her jaws. Then, as you say "bite off," bring your hands together.

The Straw, the Coal, and the Bean

A German Story from the Brothers Grimm

A woman decided to cook some beans for supper, so she started a fire in the fireplace. To make the fire burn more quickly, she threw on a handful of straw. But one piece of straw slipped out of her fingers and fell to the floor. As she put the beans in a pan to cook, one bean dropped to the floor and landed right next to the straw. Suddenly a glowing coal burst out of the fire and fell close to them.

The straw and the bean both jumped back and shouted, "Keep away! You'll burn us! What are you doing out here, anyway?"

The coal replied, "If I hadn't jumped out here, I would have been burnt to ashes by now. What are *you two* doing here?"

"Well," said the straw, "it was lucky that I slipped through the woman's fingers. Otherwise I would be nothing but smoke in her chimney right now."

Then the bean said, "Why, if that woman hadn't dropped me on the floor, I'd still be in the pot with the rest of the beans. Or maybe she would have already eaten me!"

Since they all had been so lucky to escape with their lives, they decided to travel together.

They began their journey. Soon they came to a stream with no bridge or stepping stones. The straw quickly thought of a way for them to get across. It said, "I'll lay myself over the stream. You can both walk over me as if I were a bridge."

So the straw stretched itself from bank to bank and said, "Okay, I'm ready." The bean looked at the coal. The coal looked at the bean. Then the coal, who was a bit hot-headed, bragged, "I'm not afraid to go first."

The coal began to walk boldly across the straw. But when it reached the middle of the stream, and heard the rushing water, the coal was so frightened that it froze in place! It couldn't move another step. The straw began to burn. It grew hotter and hotter until finally it broke in two and sank into the stream. The coal gave a loud hiss as it hit the water and disappeared.

When the bean saw what had happened, it laughed so hard it BURST! That would have been the end of the bean if a tailor hadn't come along. When he saw the bean with its split sides, he took out his thread and needle and sewed it up. He had only black thread with him. That is why, to this day, some beans have black seams.

About the story

Almost two hundred years ago, Jakob and Wilhelm Grimm began to gather the stories of Germany, their homeland. Their collection of stories, which we know as *Grimms' Fairy Tales,* was first published in 1812. If they had not written these stories down, many of them could have been lost forever. Among the most familiar today are "Hansel and Gretel," "Rapunzel," "Snow White," "Rumpelstiltskin," and "Sleeping Beauty."

Tips for telling

This story has a lot of action. You can make a hand movement as you say such words as "threw," "slipped," and "burst." When you say "The straw stretched itself from bank to bank," put your left hand far to your left as you say the first "bank" and then your right hand far to the right as you say the second "bank." When the coal hits the water, say the word *hiss* loudly and draw out the *s* sound at the end. When you say the coal "froze in place," freeze your body in position and look terrified.

How Brazilian Beetles Got Their Gorgeous Coats

A Story from Brazil

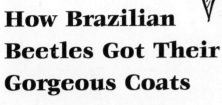

Long ago in Brazil, beetles had plain brown coats. But today their hard-shelled coats are gorgeous. They are so colorful that people often set them in pins and necklaces like precious stones. This is how it happened that Brazilian beetles got their new coats.

One day a little brown beetle was crawling along a wall. Suddenly a big gray rat darted out of a hole in the wall. When he saw the beetle, he began to make fun of her.

"Is that as fast as you can go? What a poke you are! You'll never get anywhere! Just watch how fast I can run!"

The rat dashed to the end of the wall, turned around, and ran back to the beetle. The beetle was still slowly crawling along. She had barely crawled past the spot where the rat left her.

"I'll bet you wish you could run like that!" bragged the gray rat.

"You certainly are a fast runner," replied the beetle. Even though the rat went on and on about himself, the beetle never said a word about the things she could do. She just kept slowly crawling along the wall, wishing the rat would go away.

A green and gold parrot in the mango tree above had overheard their conversation. She said to the rat, "How would you like to race with the beetle? Just to make the race exciting, I'll offer a bright colored coat as a reward. The winner may choose any color coat and I'll have it made to order."

The parrot told them the finish line would be the palm tree at the top of the hill. She gave the signal to start, and they were off.

The rat ran as fast as he could. When he reached the palm tree, he could hardly believe his eyes: there was the beetle sitting beside the parrot. The rat asked with a suspicious tone, "How did you ever manage to run fast enough to get here so soon?"

"Nobody ever said anything about having to run to win the race," replied the beetle as she drew out her tiny wings from her sides. "So I flew instead."

"I didn't know you could fly," said the rat with a grumpy look on his face.

The parrot said to the rat, "You have lost the contest. From now on you must never judge anyone by looks alone. You never can tell when or where you may find hidden wings."

Then the parrot turned to the brown beetle and asked, "What color would you like your new coat to be?"

"I'd like it to be green and gold, just like yours," replied the beetle. And since that day, Brazilian beetles have had gorgeous coats of green and gold. But the rat still wears a plain, dull, gray one.

About the story

More than 350,000 different kinds of beetles have been identified. Scientists say there are thousands, or even millions, more yet to be discovered. The beetle in the story is able to fool the rat because her shell, like all beetles' shells, is actually a pair of hardened wings.

Tips for telling

When telling any story, you need to set the mood right from the beginning. In the first sentence, make the beetle's brown coat sound boring. Then, at the end, describe her new coat with great interest and expression.

Make the rat sound like a big braggart. Hold your shoulders high and talk a little bit deeper when the rat speaks. On the other hand, when he loses the race at the end, he must sound extremely disappointed.

When the parrot advises the rat not to "judge anyone by looks alone," be sure to sound very stern. As the beetle reveals her wings at the end of the race, you may want to put your arms out to the side.

The Quarrel

A Story Told by the Cherokee Indians

Long ago, the first man and woman lived happily together for many years. But one day they had a quarrel. The woman was furious with her husband. She set off walking east, toward the sun.

The husband, who was sorry he had made his wife so mad, set off after her. But an angry woman walks quickly and does not look back. No matter how hard he tried, he could not catch up with his wife.

The husband knew how lonely he would be without her. He did not want to lose his wife. Sun saw this and offered to help the man get her back.

First, Sun made a patch of juicy blackberries appear beside the path to get the woman's attention. But the woman didn't even notice. She just kept on walking faster than ever.

Then Sun caused a bunch of blueberry bushes to spring up. Again the woman ignored them and kept on walking.

Sun thought, "I'll create a completely new fruit, one she's sure to notice." With that, Sun made a patch of juicy red strawberries appear right in the path in front of the woman.

Still she kept on walking. However, when she stepped on a ripe strawberry, she crushed it. The air was filled with a sweet fragrance.

"What's that wonderful smell?" thought the woman. She looked down and saw the luscious red fruit, the first strawberries ever. She couldn't resist. She picked one and ate it.

Mmmmmm! It was delicious. She picked another, and another. By now, Sun had cleverly caused more plants to grow behind her so that she had turned around without even realizing it. She had forgotten she was angry. She thought, "I'll pick some berries to take to my husband."

When her hands were so full that she could pick no more, she looked up and saw her husband coming in her direction. "Look what

I've found," she said as she gave him a handful of the berries. "This is the best fruit I've ever tasted."

They shared the strawberries and walked home together happily. To this day, people find it hard to argue when the sweet smell of ripe strawberries is in the air.

About the story

The name *strawberries* comes from the straw that is placed around the cultivated plant to protect the delicate berries. Most people know only the cultivated strawberry, which can be quite large. Wild strawberries are much smaller and have an even more intense taste. They grow on the ground, and when they're stepped on, as in the story, they give off a wonderful odor.

Tips for telling

Be sure to convey with your voice and body language just how furious the woman is with her husband and how sorry he feels. You may want to make a hand gesture toward the side as if to show the audience each of the berry plants Sun causes to spring up. Then make a forceful gesture with one or both hands going straight in front of you each time you say that the woman kept on walking. When Sun creates the strawberries, use your best expression so that listeners will feel as if they can smell and taste the fruit. You might want to pretend to eat a strawberry when the woman takes her first taste.

Why Parrots Only Repeat What People Say

A Story from Thailand*

Long ago, the parrot wasn't captured and taught to speak as it is today. Instead, people brought the lorikeet, the parrot's cousin, to live in their homes. Back then, the lorikeet was able to repeat what it heard and speak its own thoughts. Unfortunately, as you'll see from this story, that got the lorikeet into a lot of trouble.

There was once a man who owned a magnificent lorikeet. One day, the man stole his neighbor's water buffalo. When he was questioned by his neighbor, the lorikeet's owner replied, "I have no idea what happened to your water buffalo."

But the lorikeet knew the truth. It called out, "Brrrk! Master stole it. Master killed it. Brrrk! Master ate part. Hid the rest in the rice bins. Brrrk!"

Sure enough, when the neighbor checked in the rice bins, there was the buffalo meat. The man claimed he was innocent, but his lorikeet kept calling out, "Brrrk! Master stole it. Master killed it. Brrrk! Master ate part. Hid the rest in the rice bins. Brrrk!" At last the neighbor said, "We'll settle this in court tomorrow."

The lorikeet's owner realized he must come up with a plan to avoid going to jail. That night, he put the lorikeet's cage in a big box. For hours he beat on the box with a stick and poured water over it.

*Thailand is pronounced TIE-land.

Although it was a beautiful evening, the poor lorikeet thought it was in the midst of a terrible storm.

The next day in court, the judge demanded to know what had happened to the water buffalo. Once again, the lorikeet called out, "Brrrk! Master stole it. Master killed it. Brrrk! Master ate part. Hid the rest in the rice bins. Brrrk!" When the judge heard this, he ordered, "Take this man to jail!"

Before the guards could take him away, the man pleaded with the judge, "Your honor, please give me a chance to defend myself. You see, this bird loves to lie. Ask my lorikeet something else. Ask it what the weather was like last night."

When the judge asked the question, the lorikeet replied, "Brrrk! Dreadful night. Thunder rumbled. Rain poured. Brrrk! Never so scared in my life! Brrrk!"

"You see, your honor," said the man, "the bird loves to tell stories."

The guilty man was allowed to go free. When he got home with the lorikeet, he opened the cage and said angrily, "Go on! Fly away! I don't want to see you in my house ever again!"

Since that time, people have not kept lorikeets as pets. When the lorikeet returned to the jungle, it met a new bird, the parrot. The lorikeet noticed the parrot's beautiful feathers and special voice. It knew people soon would want to take parrots into their homes.

The lorikeet warned the parrot, "Brrrk! Don't speak your own mind! You'll get in a lot of trouble. Brrrk! Only repeat what people say. They love to hear their own thoughts. Brrrk!"

Sure enough, the lorikeet was right. Today the parrot is a favorite pet in many homes. And it still remembers the lorikeet's warning. That's why the parrot never says what it thinks. It just repeats what people say.

About the story

The shape of the parrot's tongue and beak allow it to make sounds very similar to human speech. Although parrots are very social, they do not imitate other sounds when living in the wild, but only in captivity. Scientists think this is because parrots quickly learn the sounds around them and find that repeating these sounds brings a great deal of attention. This becomes a substitute for their normal social life in the wild.

Tips for telling

Your listeners will really enjoy this story if you squawk and pretend to talk like a bird when the lorikeet speaks. Remember, if your listeners laugh, it's because they're laughing *with* you, not *at* you!

When you describe how the lorikeet's owner tried to fool the bird, pretend to beat on an imaginary box and then pour water over it. Make the owner sound furious when he returns home from court, opens the cage, and sends the lorikeet away.

The Taxi Ride

A Story from Northern Ghana and Mauritania*

If you go for a drive in the country and happen to see a donkey in the road, chances are he'll just stand there. Even if you honk your horn at him, he'll stare at you as if you're crazy and keep standing right in your way. If you meet a goat, he always seems to scurry away as fast as he can. And if you see a dog near the road, he will often chase your car. The people of West Africa have a story to explain why these animals behave the way they do.

You see, some time ago, when cars first came to the roads, a donkey, a goat, and a dog took a ride in a taxi. They needed to get home to the villages where they lived.

When they reached the first village, the donkey tapped the driver on the shoulder and said, "This is where I get out. How much do I owe you?"

"Five coins," said the driver.

The donkey paid and got out. The taxi driver drove on down the road with the goat and the dog. Soon the goat tapped the driver on the shoulder and said, "This is my village. How much?"

"Five coins," said the driver.

The goat didn't have enough money with him. He jumped out of the taxi and scampered away without paying the driver.

*Ghana is pronounced *GAH-na.*
  Mauritania is pronounced
  maw-rih-TANE-e-ah.

At long last, they came to the dog's village. He tapped the driver on the shoulder and asked, "How much?"

"Five coins," said the driver.

The dog got out of the car, took out his bag of coins, and began to count. Suddenly the driver grabbed the whole bag of coins and drove off down the road, roaring with laughter.

So now you know why a donkey, a goat, and a dog all do different things when a car comes down the road.

Donkeys just stand right where they are. They let the driver go around them. They know they've paid up. They've done nothing wrong, so they've got nothing to be ashamed of.

When a goat sees a car coming, it'll scamper off as fast as it can. It knows it didn't pay the taxi fare and the driver is still looking for his money.

But dogs spend their time chasing cars. They're still trying to find the taxi driver who once cheated them.

About the story

This story was told to Michael Butcher a few years ago while he was working for Oxfam in West Africa. Oxfam is an international organization that aids poor people living in very difficult conditions. Many of them have rich storytelling traditions that are still alive to this day, partly because electricity is scarce along with televisions and radios. So people tell and listen to stories, using their creativity and imaginations while building strong bonds with each other.

Tips for telling

Pretend to tap someone on the shoulder each time one of the animals is ready to get out of the taxi. When the goat gets out, emphasize *jumped* and *scampered* and make appropriate hand gestures at the same time. When it's the dog's turn, pretend to take out a bag of coins and start to count them. Then make a grabbing motion as the driver steals the bag from the dog.

Don't rush the ending. Emphasizing the word *still* in the last sentence will help slow you down.

How Owl Got His Feathers

A Story from Puerto Rico

Long ago, the animals gave large parties and balls. Everyone was invited. They wore their finest outfits and had a great time dancing and feasting.

One day, the birds decided to have a grand ball. They wanted every bird to be there. They sent Hawk to knock on all the birds' doors to invite them.

When Hawk got to Owl's house and gave him the invitation, Owl was worried. You see, back then Owl did not have feathers. Owl said, "All the other birds will be there in their fine feather suits. They'll make fun of me. I can't possibly go."

Hawk told the other birds what Owl had said. They decided each one of them would lend Owl a feather so that he could have a fine suit of feathers and come to the ball. Hawk collected the feathers of different colors and gave them to Owl. He warned Owl that each feather had to be returned to its owner after the party.

Owl arranged the feathers very carefully. Everyone at the ball agreed that Owl looked quite handsome in his new suit. He was so pleased. But during the ball he kept thinking about how he would look when it was over. He hated the thought of having to return the feathers. So when no one was looking, he stole away from the ball and hid in the forest.

When the party was over, the other birds looked for Owl so they could get their feathers back. But he was nowhere to be seen.

To this day, Owl still wears that same fine suit, and the other birds are still looking for him. That is why Owl is never seen by day. He comes out only at night when other birds are sleeping.

About the story

The owl's downy feathers make its flight silent. This allows the bird to hear creatures moving around and makes the owl less likely to disturb prey as it moves in for the kill. Feathers circling an owl's eyes also help its hearing. They pick up sounds and direct them to the ears, hidden just behind. Most owls hunt only at night, using their very large eyes to see in the dark.

Tips for telling

When you describe how the animals wore their finest outfits, you may want to hold your shoulders high and use both hands to show your fine imaginary clothes. But when Owl tells Hawk that he won't go to the dance because the other birds will make fun of him, slump your shoulders and sound very worried.

Two Brothers, Two Rewards

A Story told in China, Korea, and Japan

Long ago, there were two brothers who were as different as could be. Everything came easily to the older brother. He was able to save a great fortune without a great deal of work. But despite all his wealth, he was an unhappy man who always wanted more.

His younger brother, on the other hand, had no luck when it came to making money, but managed to be happy with the little he had. The oldest brother thought him a fool and never helped out, even though he had plenty of money for both of them.

One day, the younger brother found a sparrow with a broken wing. He took the bird home and nursed it back to health. By springtime the sparrow was strong enough to fly on its own. The brother took the bird out to his garden and said, "Go on, little bird, it's time for you to fly home to your family." Much to his amazement, the sparrow replied, "You have been very kind to me. Even though you expected nothing in return, please take this pumpkin seed as a reward. Plant it in your garden and wait for it to ripen."

The younger brother planted the seed and watered it carefully. Soon a pumpkin vine sprouted out of the ground. By summer's end, the vine was filled with beautiful orange pumpkins. When he cut one open, gold and silver and diamonds poured out! Every one of the pumpkins was filled with the same riches. He was now the wealthiest man in town.

The news of his poor brother's sudden fortune reached the older brother. He didn't want anyone—and certainly not his younger brother—to have more money than he had. Going quickly to his brother's house, he demanded to know how he had become rich so suddenly. The younger brother didn't like to lie, so he told him all about the sparrow he had nursed back to health.

The older brother was determined to get his own reward. So the next day, he went into the woods to find a wounded sparrow. He couldn't find one, so he took out his slingshot, shot a sparrow, and broke its wing. He rushed over to pick up the bird and said, "Oh, you poor thing! Come back to my house and I'll take care of your injuries. But if I nurse you back to health, you must give me a reward."

The older brother was very good to the sparrow, but not because he was kindhearted. The sooner it got better, he thought, the sooner he'd get his reward. At last the bird had enough strength to fly away. The older brother said to it, "Go on, return to your family. But before you go, I expect to get my reward."

The sparrow replied, "Don't worry. I would never forget to give you something in return. Please take this pumpkin seed. Plant it in your garden and wait for it to ripen."

The older brother planted the seed right away. As he watered the plant he thought, "It won't be long before I'm richer than my brother once again!"

He was surprised to see that the plant did not grow along the ground. Instead, it grew straight up. Higher and higher it grew until it seemed that it had reached the moon. But he wondered why there were no pumpkins to be seen. He thought, "I'll bet my reward will be even greater than my brother's. I'll climb up and collect all the gold and silver of the moon. When I return, I'll be the richest man in the whole land!"

The older brother began to climb and climb and climb. When at last he reached the moon and stepped onto it, the vine disappeared! And if you look up into the sky on any moonlit night, you'll see that he's still up there, for the greedy man has lived all alone on the moon ever since.

About the story

Every culture seems to have one or more stories about the spots or markings on the moon. The markings are caused by the way the moon's surface reflects sunlight. The dark shadows are actually places where molten rock poured out long ago. These areas do not reflect sunlight as well as the mountainous regions.

It would be impossible for human beings to live on the moon for many reasons. To start with, temperatures there are extreme. The moon's days and nights each last fourteen Earth days. While the sun shines on the moon, the surface temperature is hot enough to boil water. But during the fourteen-day "night," the moon is dark and much colder than ice.

Tips for telling

Show the great difference between these two brothers by using your voice and face, as well as body movements. Have a scowl on your face and a nasty tone in your voice whenever the older, greedy brother speaks. From the time he receives his pumpkin seed from the sparrow, have his greediness build and build. Pretend to look up into the sky and see the vine stretching all the way to the moon. Make him sound extremely greedy and very excited at the end when he thinks he's going to climb the vine and collect riches.

Why Bear Has a Stumpy Tail

A Story from Norway

One cold winter morning, Fox stole a long string of fish from a fisherman's cart. As she was on her way back to her den, she met Bear. Bear's eyes grew big when he saw the fish. His tail began to swing back and forth in excitement. You see, this was a long time ago when bears had long, bushy tails instead of the short, stumpy ones they have today.

Bear said to Fox, "Goodness! What a tasty-looking catch you have there! Would you share it with me?"

"No!" Fox snapped. "These are *my* fish. It took a long time to catch them. If you want some, you'll have to catch them yourself."

Bear asked with a suspicious tone, "How did you catch them? The water's frozen solid."

With a sly gleam in her eye, Fox replied, "Why, just come with me, Bear. I'll be glad to show you."

Fox led Bear down to the lake and said, "It's easy, Bear. First, you must cut a hole in the ice. Then stick your tail in. Hold it there as long as you can. It will hurt when the fish grab on, but the longer you hold it there, the more fish you'll catch. When you think you've caught enough, just give a strong, hard pull."

Bear did just what Fox had told him. Soon he felt what he thought was

a bite. "You're right, Fox!" he cried excitedly. "I'm already catching fish."

Fox ran off laughing to herself. She knew what Bear was feeling was the water beginning to freeze around his tail.

Bear sat there all afternoon. His tail hurt more and more, but he was determined to catch as many fish as Fox. Finally, Bear decided he'd caught enough. He tried to pull his tail out of the ice, but it wouldn't budge. He gave another hard pull. Still nothing happened. At last Bear pulled so hard that his tail broke off! Most of Bear's bushy tail was still stuck in the ice. All that was left was the little stumpy tail that bears have to this day.

Bear roared with pain. He cried out, "Wait till I get my hands on that no-good, lying Fox!" He dashed off to find her. What happened when Bear finally caught up to Fox?...That's another story!

About the story

This is one of the most famous animal stories told throughout Europe. It was so popular that it spread to Africa and the Americas— even to some places where bears do not live and the water does not freeze!

The cleverness of the fox has been celebrated in the myths and fables of the world for hundreds of years. This trickster reputation is well deserved. Foxes do have an uncanny ability to outwit their enemies.

Tips for telling

You must show in your telling that Fox is a sly trickster and that Bear is willing to believe anything Fox tells him in order to get some fish. At the beginning when Bear meets Fox, make your eyes big and look very excited as you describe Bear's reaction to seeing the fish.

At the end of the story, use movements and voice expression to show how Bear struggles to pull his tail out of the ice. You may want to make a quick motion with both hands as you say the words "broke off!"

After you ask, "What happened when Bear finally caught up to Fox?" be sure to pause before saying, "That's another story!" This will trick your audience into thinking you're about to tell them more.

Where All Stories Come From

A Story told by the Seneca Indians*

Long ago, there was a Seneca boy who set off each morning to hunt in the forest. He would return home at the end of the day with birds or other small game to help feed his family. One afternoon, the boy climbed on a large stone to rest. As he sat there, he heard a voice say, "Would you like to hear a story?"

The boy was startled. He looked all around but didn't see anyone. Again the voice said, "Would you like to hear a story?" At last the boy realized it was the stone he was sitting on that had spoken. The boy replied, "What does it mean to tell a story?"

The stone said, "It is when you tell about things that happened a long time ago."

"Sure. That sounds like fun," said the boy. "Please—tell me a story."

"First, you must give me one of the birds you caught today," said the stone.

The boy laid down one of the birds, and the stone began to tell a story of the way things used to be. It told about strange creatures, called stone giants and flying heads, that used to make war on the Seneca people. When the stone finished one story, it began another.

All afternoon, the stone told stories. The

*Seneca is pronounced
SEN-uh-kah
(SEN rhymes with BEN).

boy was spellbound by the tales. At last, as the sun began to set, the stone said, "That's enough for today. Come back tomorrow and I will tell you more, but be sure to bring another bird."

The boy did as he was told. The next day he listened to stories until it once again began to grow dark. As the weeks passed by, the boy brought other people from his village with him. Soon a great number of people came to listen to the amazing stories told by the stone.

At last one day, the stone said to the boy, "I no longer will tell you stories. It is now your job to remember them and tell them to your people. Wherever you go to tell these legends, you will be welcomed and cared for."

The boy never forgot the stories. In every Seneca village where he told them, he was given gifts, just as he had given the stone a gift each day. He spread the stories among the Seneca people until he died. The tales are still told to this day.

About the story

The Seneca are one of the six tribes of the Iroquois Confederacy, which also included the Mohawk, Oneida, Onondaga, Cayuga, and Tuscarora. The Iroquois storyteller always carried a mysterious bag filled with feathers, bones, arrowheads, and other items. Each represented a story. A small stone probably would have been placed in the bag as a reminder of this tale.

The Iroquois told their stories during the cold winter months. They felt the tales were so powerful that, if they told them during the growing season, even the corn and beans and other plants would stop to listen.

Tips for telling

When the boy first hears the voice, pretend to look around with a confused look on your face. You may want to make your voice a little deeper, and perhaps a bit louder, each time the stone speaks. Have a puzzled look on your face when the boy asks, "What does it mean to tell a story?"

General Tips for Telling Stories

As we mentioned in the introduction, you will find that the stories in this book are great fun to read aloud. They are folktales—stories passed down by word of mouth from one generation to the next. In many cases, they were told for hundreds of years before being written down. These stories are meant to be *heard*, and they will have the most impact when they are shared just as they used to be—told from memory, without a book, by one person to another.

If you're reading this section, it's probably because you have seen someone tell stories. Perhaps you were amazed by how captivating it can be to hear a person tell a story without props, costumes, or any special effects. Storytelling is as old as the world, and yet even in our age of television, movies, and computer games, it can be a powerful experience. As a story is told, listeners see pictures in their minds. These pictures differ as people use their own imaginations, making storytelling a very personal experience. But it is also a bonding time because there is always a sense that the audience has shared the same adventure.

You may be thinking, "It sounds like a lot of work to learn a story to tell. I'll bet it will be as good if I read it out loud." Not really. Just pick the story you enjoyed most and try telling it. You will find there is a big difference between reading a story to someone and telling it without the book. Without a text in hand, the storyteller is free to use facial expressions and body movements to make the telling more interesting. Your listeners will show much better attention and enjoyment of the story when you lay the book aside and put your heart into the story. As they listen to your words and watch your expression and movement, the story will spring to life for them.

If you would like to give storytelling a try, here are a few tips to get you started.

CHOOSING A STORY

Pick a story you *really* enjoy.

Although all the stories in this book are good for telling, you must be sure to choose one that really appeals to *you*. Your enthusiasm for the story is very important. When you love a story, your listeners sense your excitement and are swept along by your telling. If the storyteller sees and feels the places, characters, and events in the story, the listeners will as well.

If you have never told a story before, be sure to pick a short, simple one for your first telling. Once you are successful and see how much fun it can be, you can move on to more complicated stories. The more stories you tell, the more you'll discover what your strengths are. You may find that you're terrific at telling a nature myth or ghost story or that you're especially good at making people laugh. Perhaps you're good at all of them!

Consider who your audience will be.

Before you choose a story, think about the listeners. For your first experience, it may be easiest to tell to young kids. If they are very young children, you must pick a story appropriate for them. Forget about those scary stories you love; save them for your peers. Some little ones frighten easily. Look for stories that are simple and straightforward. Young children love stories with a lot of repetition, and you can encourage them to join in on repeated phrases.

If you plan to tell the story for listeners your own age, the process of choosing is much easier. If you pick a story that you enjoy, more than likely your friends will enjoy it also.

LEARNING A STORY

Find a way of learning the story that works for you.

Many find it helpful to begin by doing a storyboard or cartoon drawing of the story. Sketch simple stick figures and scenes from the story, placing them in boxes, one after the other, to represent the tale's main events. The point is to help you learn the story, not to produce a work of art. If you prefer, you can make a written outline instead.

Next, try telling the story using your storyboard or outline. Begin by telling the story to yourself. Whenever possible, tell it out loud. Once you feel you know the story, put aside the storyboard or outline. This will help you get beyond simply memorizing to making the story your own. Be sure to go back and look at the original tale now and then to be sure you're not leaving out any important events or clever wordings.

Some tellers also find it very helpful to tell or read the story into a tape recorder, and then listen to it until they feel they know it.

Tell the story again and again.

As soon as you're sure you remember the basic plot, tell it to someone else the first chance you get. Tell it to a friend while you're riding the school bus or to your family during dinner. Telling over and over helps you find what makes a story work—the details, voices, and expressions that bring it alive. Ask your listeners for suggestions. If they say they had a hard time telling the difference between characters or that you spoke too quickly, you'll know what to work on. The more people you try it out on, the better, because every listener will notice different things.

It's also very helpful to practice in front of a mirror and to try out movements and facial expressions that will enhance the story.

Make the story your own.

Remember that the stories in this book represent other cultures. We encourage you to tell them in your own way, but you can't just change them around as you please and say they still represent a certain culture. When you first find a story you think you'd like to tell, make sure you feel comfortable with every part of it. If there's something that seems silly to you, you must ask yourself: can I change this part of the story in a way that won't harm the meaning? If the answer is "no," it's best to find a different tale to tell.

It's also wise to visit the library and read some background on the customs and ways of the people whose story you've chosen. You may learn interesting details that you could share with listeners in your introduction to the tale. But even if you don't mention what you've learned, you will do a better job of telling because you understand something about the original tellers.

Be sure to see the map on page 12 that shows where the people who told the stories in this book come from.

TELLING A STORY

To learn to be a good teller, watch other storytellers whenever you get the chance.

The best way to learn to tell stories is to observe as many storytellers as possible. Begin by paying close attention to friends, family members, classmates, teachers, or characters in a movie or television show. We are all storytellers, and some folks seem to come by their talents naturally. Carefully watch the people you love to listen to. Listen to their voices, watch their facial expressions, and observe their body movements. What is it they do that keeps your interest?

Try to observe some professional storytellers, if possible. These are people who get a lot of practice telling stories because they do it for a living. There are *many* different styles of telling. Watching a variety of storytellers will help you to see the possibilities and find a style you feel comfortable with. If you can't see a storyteller's performance in person, ask if your local library owns any videos of professional tellers.

Take your time—but don't go on *too* long!

When you tell your story, remember that you have the floor! The feeling that you are standing in front of a group of people with all eyes on you is both scary and very exciting. The adrenaline or extra energy that people often feel in this situation makes some tellers rush through a story. You can't really do justice to a tale if you speak too quickly. Listeners should be able to relax and enjoy a story, which is tough to do if the teller is talking a mile a minute. Slow down. Take your time.

On the other hand, don't dawdle, and never make the story longer than it needs to be. Take your cues from your listeners. This is good advice for everyday communication in general. You want listeners to look bright-eyed and interested. If they start to seem bored, you'll know you're going on too long and need to wrap it up.

Be expressive!

Although there are many important tips to keep in mind as you tell a story, the most important is to put expression or feeling in your voice, on your face, and in your body movements. If you are telling "The Quarrel," for example, you must let your listeners know just how furious the woman is. Sound angry, have an angry look on your face, and also show the anger in your body. If you are telling "Two Brothers, Two Rewards," you really must show a *difference* between the kind and greedy brothers. Nothing will bore an audience faster than a story told without expression.

Vary your voice!

There are many ways to change your voice. For example, although you must always speak loudly and clearly enough for everyone to hear, you would probably speak in a quieter voice when a character is scared or embarrassed. On the other hand, you might get loud when a character is angry or excited.

You should also vary the pitch of your voice. A low, deep pitch would be appropriate for a big bully or a monster. A higher pitch might be used for a tiny creature such as a mouse. Most characters would speak in a higher-pitched voice when they are excited or frightened. For example, think about how your voice might sound if you screamed "Help!"

Changing the speed or tempo of your voice can help create different moods and make the story interesting. If one character is chasing another, you would want to show the excitement by speaking more quickly during that part. At the beginning of "Why Cats Wash Their Paws After Eating," the teller should speak very slowly as she says, "She crept toward it slowly and quietly, and kept very close to the ground." Right afterward, she should speak quickly as she says, "Then she pounced on the bird and grabbed it between her paws."

Don't be afraid of silence.

Every second of your story should *not* be filled with sound. Some of the most effective times in a story are when the teller pauses and there is complete silence. If, for example, a character opens the lid of a trunk filled with gold, pause and pretend to see the box's contents before you tell the listeners what's inside. Be sure to show the appropriate expression on your face in response to the gold.

Use a distinct character voice when necessary.

You will find that some characters in your story need special voices. If you choose to tell "Why Parrots Only Repeat What People Say," it's very important that you feel comfortable imitating a parrot voice. The story just won't work without it.

As you are learning your story, think about your characters. If you are telling "Why the Farmer and the Bear are Enemies," walk around the room the way you think the bear would walk. Hold your shoulders high and look mean and tough. Then try some voices until you find the way you think the bear would talk. Letting your body feel like the character will help you to find a good voice. When you've figured out the bear's voice, use the same process for the farmer.

Use sound effects when appropriate.

Stories tend to be full of lots of interesting noises—doors creaking, wind blowing, babies crying. If you are good at imitating, such sounds can sometimes be used to enhance a story.

Use gestures and body movements to help listeners see pictures in their minds.

Gestures and body movements can help a story come alive. But any movements you make must help listeners see pictures in their minds. Simple movements, mostly from your waist up, will help your audience make visual images. If you get carried away and do too much movement, they will see only you and may lose the thread of the story. Take, for example, this action-packed sentence: "She hit the ball, ran to first, and slid into second." If you took a big, exaggerated swing, ran across the room, and then slid on the floor, you most likely would get a laugh. However, your listeners probably would have forgotten about the story. Remember, you're not in a play. Instead of really acting out the scene, stand in one place, facing the audience. As you say "hit," take a controlled swing and then run in place as you say "ran." As you say "slid," use one hand to make a quick sliding motion out toward the audience. The listeners will be able to see your face well and will be able to picture the busy scene clearly in their heads.

Look at your listeners.

It is very important that you maintain eye contact with your listeners throughout the story. A storyteller who looks down at the floor or above the heads of the audience will find it hard to keep people's attention. When one character speaks to another, make the listeners be the other character. For example, when the hawk in "Why Hens Scratch in the Dirt" says to the hen, "You're lying to me," look right at the audience as if you are the hawk and they are the hen.

It is sometimes very effective to pretend to "see" a person or an object as you tell the story. For example, at the end of "The Dancing Brothers," you can pretend to see the pine tree growing straight up into the sky and then the brothers dancing. If you convince your listeners that you see these things with your eyes, they will picture them as well.

Put expression on your face!

A good way to find out if you are putting the right expression on your face is to practice in a mirror. If a character is angry, you shouldn't be smiling.

One of the hardest challenges for many tellers is not to laugh at themselves when they tell in front of a group. For example, if a teller uses a terrific scared expression and the audience responds by laughing, the teller sometimes laughs, too. Remember to stay right in the story and keep looking scared. It's the listeners' job to laugh, not yours.

Try to include audience participation whenever appropriate.

Younger children love repetition. If a phrase is repeated again and again in a story, have them join in. After you say the phrase the first time, ask your listeners, "Why don't you do that with me?" Then do it again immediately so they can practice. When it comes around the next time, motion to them so they'll remember to join in.

Use your nervous energy to make the story better.

Being nervous is a sign that you have extra energy. Contrary to what you might think, this is good. Any performer or athlete needs extra energy.

What's important is to use it in a positive way to improve your telling. The more energy you add, the better your storytelling will be.

There are two things you can do to help deal with nervousness. The first is to be well prepared. The more you practice, the more confident you will feel. It's a lot like taking a test in school. If you have studied the material, you know you will do your best. The second thing is to just do it! Your most difficult telling will be your first. Every time you face a group of listeners, it will feel a little easier. You will know the story better and be able to anticipate the listeners' reactions. Then you can really start to have fun with your story.

As one of our young storytellers said, "I thought I would be terrible at storytelling. But after I told my story, I felt great. I realized I could do something I never thought I could do. I won't be so afraid to try new things from now on."

Pass these stories on!

Tell the stories in this book whenever you get a chance. You could tell them at the dinner table to entertain your family or during a long car ride while on summer vacation. You also could tell them in front of your classmates at school. If you have to do an oral report on a country and would like to make it more interesting for the class, try telling a story as part of it. If you baby-sit for younger children, you will find there's no better way of entertaining them than telling stories. If you go camping or have a sleep-over with friends or a family reunion, those are also perfect times for telling tales.

So take the risk! Try telling a story, whether it's to a friend sitting on your front porch or to your whole class at school. As one ten-year-old storyteller said, "What matters most is having fun. You lighten everyone up by telling a story."

Activities

Here are some fun activities you may want to do after you've read or told these stories.

1. If any of these tales made you think, "No! That's not how it happened at all. I know the *real* reason...," that's great! Make up your own story to explain anything the stories in this book explain. For example, you may have your own ideas about "How Tigers Got Their Stripes" or "Why Hens Scratch in the Dirt."

   If you come up with a good story, send it to us. We may be interested in having other kids tell it, or we may want to include it in a future book of "how and why" stories. Send your story via e-mail to:

   bnb@clarityconnect.com

   or via snail mail to:

   Beauty & the Beast Storytellers
   Martha Hamilton and Mitch Weiss
   954 Coddington Road
   Ithaca, NY 14850

   Be sure to tell us how to contact you if we decide to use the story so we can get written permission from you.

2. Here are lots of titles that may give you ideas for even more stories:

Why Mole Lives Underground

Why the Owl Has Big Eyes

Why Dogs Howl at the Moon

Why Snake Has No Feet or Hands

How Camel Got His Hump

Why Pigs Grunt

Why Geese Fly in a V

Why Cats Have Nine Lives

Why Red Pepper is So Hot

Why Rabbit Has Long Ears and a Short Tail

Why Birds Have Many Colors

Why Snails Have Shells

Why Zebras Have Stripes

Why Roses Have Thorns

Why Pigs Have Curly Tails

Where Socks Go When They Disappear in the Wash

Why the Snail is So Slow

How Elephant Got His Long Trunk

Why There are Rainbows

Why Whales Spout

How Giraffe Got His Long Neck

How Deer Got His Antlers

Why Cats' Eyes Glow in the Dark

Why Bulls Hate Red

Why Opossums Hang By Their Tails

How Rattlesnakes Got Their Rattles

Why the Moon Changes Shape

Why Trees Lose Their Leaves in the Fall

How the Jellyfish Came to Be

Why the Tide Goes In and Out

3. Every place has its own local stories. The area where we live in central New York State is called the Finger Lakes region. If you look at a map, you will see there are many long, thin lakes that resemble fingers. The Native Americans from our area, the Iroquois Indians, say the Great Spirit put his hand down on the earth and caused these lakes to be formed.

    Go to your library and ask how you can find out about "how and why" stories from your area. If you have a local historical association, they may be able to help you.

4. If you would like to read more scientific explanations of "how and why," look for these books at your local library or bookstore:

Ardley, Bridget, and Neil Ardley. *The Random House Book of 1001 Questions and Answers.* NY: Random House, 1989.

Campbell, Ann-Jeannette, and Ronald Road. *The New York Public Library Incredible Earth: A Book of Answers for Kids.* NY: John Wiley, 1996.

Ganeri, Anita. *I Wonder Why Camels Have Humps and Other Questions About Animals.* NY: Kingfisher, 1993.

The Kingfisher Illustrated Encyclopedia of Animals. NY: Kingfisher, 1992.

National Geographic Society. *National Geographic Book of Mammals.* Washington, DC: National Geographic Society, 1998.

O'Neill, Amanda. *I Wonder Why Spiders Spin Webs and Other Questions About Creepy Crawlers.* NY: Kingfisher, 1995.

Pope, Joyce. *Do Animals Dream?: Children's Questions About Animals Most Often Asked of the Natural History Museum.* NY: Viking Kestrel, 1986.

Settel, Joanne, and Nancy Baggett. *Why Do Cats' Eyes Glow in the Dark? (And Other Questions Kids Ask About Animals).* NY: Atheneum, 1988.

Staple, Michele, and Linda Gamlin. *The Random House Book of 1001 Questions and Answers About Animals.* NY: Random House, 1990.

Stott, Carole. *I Wonder Why Stars Twinkle and Other Questions About Space.* NY: Kingfisher, 1993.

Taylor, Charles, and Stephen Pople. *The Oxford Children's Book of Science.* NY: Oxford Univ. Press, 1995.

Whitfield, Philip, and Joyce Pope. *Why Do the Seasons Change?: Questions on Nature's Cycles and Rhythms Answered by the Natural History Museum.* NY: Viking Kestrel, 1987.

Wood, Jenny. *I Wonder Why Kangaroos Have Pouches and Other Questions About Baby Animals.* NY: Kingfisher, 1996.

5. If you would like to read more "how and why" stories, check for these books at the library. Some may be hard to find.

Greaves, Nick. *When Hippo Was Hairy and Other Tales from Africa*. NY: Barrons, 1988.

Hamilton, Virginia. *In the Beginning: Creation Stories from Around the World*. NY: Harcourt Brace Jovanovich, 1988.

Kipling, Rudyard. *Just So Stories*. NY: William Morrow, 1996.

Leach, Maria. *How the People Sang the Mountains Up: How and Why Stories*. NY: Viking, 1967.

Mayo, Margaret. *When the World Was Young: Creation and Pourquoi Tales*. NY: Simon & Schuster, 1996.

6. If you would like some more good stories to read and tell, see our award-winning book and tape entitled *Stories in My Pocket: Tales Kids Can Tell* (Fulcrum Publishers, 1996; 1-800-992-2908). Those who teach storytelling may be interested in *Children Tell Stories: a Teaching Guide* (Richard C. Owen Publishers, 1990; 1-800-336-5588). Both books and the tape are also available through our website at:

www.clarityconnect.com/webpages3/bnb/

or by writing to us at the address on page 87.

Story Sources

Other versions of stories we have retold in this book may be found in the following sources:

Thunder and Lightning
"The Story of the Lightning and the Thunder," in *Folk Stories from Southern Nigeria West Africa*, by Elphinstone Dayrell (London: Longmans, Green & Co., 1910), 70-71.

The Story of Thunder and Lightning, by Ashley Bryan (NY: Atheneum, 1993).

How Tigers Got Their Stripes
"The Tiger's Stripes," in *The Toad is the Emperor's Uncle: Animal Folktales from Vietnam*, by Vo-Dinh (Garden City, NY: Doubleday, 1970), 65-73.

"How the Tiger Got His Stripes," in *Vietnamese Legends*, adapted by George F. Schultz (Rutland, VT: Charles E. Tuttle, 1965), 15-18.

The following Thai variant has many similarities:

"Why the Tiger is Striped," in *Tales from Thailand*, as told by Marian Davies Toth (Rutland, VT: Charles E. Tuttle, 1971), 85-90.

Why Bat Flies Alone at Night
"War Between Beasts and Birds," in *Myths of the Modocs*, by Jeremiah Curtin (Boston: Little, Brown, 1912), 213.

The Mill at the Bottom of the Sea
"Why the Sea is Salty," in *Korean Folk and Fairy Tales*, by Suzanne Crowder Han (Elizabeth, NJ: Hollym, 1991), 228-30. Adapted by permission of the author.

Why Cats Wash Their Paws After Eating
"Why Cat Eats First and Washes Afterward," in *The Lion Sneezed: Folktales and Myths of the Cat*, by Maria Leach (NY: Crowell, 1977), 13. (Leach says there also are numerous African variants of this story.)

"Why Cats Always Wash Themselves After Eating," in *Once Upon a Time*, by Rose Dobbs (NY: Random House, 1950), 67-69.

"Why the Cat Washes His Paws After Eating," in *Catlore: Tales from Around the World*, retold by Marjorie Zaum (NY: Atheneum, 1985), 43-44.

Why Ants are Found Everywhere
"Why Ants Are Found Everywhere," in *The Burman: His Life and Customs*, by Shway Yoe (London: Macmillan, 1896), 563.

Why Frog and Snake Never Play Together
"Why Frog and Snake Never Play Together," in *In the Shadow of the Bush*, by P. Amaury Talbot (London: William Heinemann, 1912), 386.

"Why Frog and Snake Never Play Together," in *Beat the Story-Drum, Pum-Pum*, by Ashley Bryan (NY: Macmillan, 1980), 41-52.

Why the Baby Says "Goo"
"How the Lord of Men and Beasts Strove With the Mighty Wasis, and Was Shamefully Defeated," in *The Algonquin Legends of New England*, by Charles G. Leland (Boston: Houghton Mifflin, 1885), 120-22.

"Why the Baby Says 'Goo,'" in *Myths of the Red Children*, by Gilbert L. Wilson (NY: Ginn & Co., 1907), 87-92.

"Glooskap," in *A Cavalcade of Goblins*, by Alan Garner (NY: Walck, 1969), 210-12.

"Glooskap and the Baby," in *Myths and Legends: The North American Indians*, by Lewis Spence (Boston: David D. Nickerson & Co., 1914), 145-46.

Why the Farmer and the Bear are Enemies
"The Peasant and the Bear," in *Baba Yaga's Geese and Other Russian Stories*, by Bonnie Carey (Bloomington: Indiana University Press, 1973), 84-85.

"The Peasant and the Bear," in *Three Rolls and One Doughnut: Fables from Russia*, retold by Mirra Ginsburg (NY: Dial, 1970), 27-29.

"The Peasant, the Bear, and the Fox," in *Tales from Atop a Russian Stove*, by Janet Higonnet-Schnopper (Chicago: Albert Whitman & Co., 1973), 76-81.

Why Hens Scratch in the Dirt
"The Cock and the Sparrow-Hawk," in *Filipino Popular Tales*, collected by Dean S. Fansler (Hatboro, PA: Folklore Association, 1965), 415-16.

"The Cock and the Sparrow-Hawk," in *Once in the First Times: Folk Tales from the Philippines*, by Elizabeth Hough Sechrist (Philadelphia: Macrae Smith Co., 1949), 25-27.

"Why the Hen Scratches all the Time," in *Tales from the Mountain Province*, retold by I.V. Mallari (Manila: Philippine Education Co., 1958), 48-50.

"The Lost Necklace," in *Filipino Popular Tales*, collected by Dean S. Fansler (Hatboro, PA: Folklore Association, 1965), 414-15.

Why the Sun Comes Up When Rooster Crows

"Rooster and the Nine Suns," in *Why Snails Have Shells: Minority and Han Folktales from China* (Hani variant), retold by Carolyn Han (Honolulu: Univ. of Hawaii, 1993), 16-18.

"How the Cock Got His Red Crown," in *Favorite Children's Stories from China and Tibet* (Miao variant), by Lotta Carswell Hume (Rutland, VT: Charles E. Tuttle, 1962), 27-32.

"Why the Sun Rises When the Rooster Crows," in *The Magic Boat and Other Chinese Folk Stories* (Hani variant), by M.A. Jagendorf and Virginia Weng (NY: Vanguard, 1980), 87-91.

Why Dogs Chase Cats

Mules and Men, by Zora Neale Hurston (NY: Negro Universities Press, 1935), 101-02.

"Why Dogs Hate Cats," in *The Knee-High Man and Other Tales*, by Julius Lester (NY: Dial, 1972), 9-10.

The Dancing Brothers

"Origin of the Constellations," in "Myths of the Iroquois," by Erminnie A. Smith, U. S. Bureau of American Ethnology, *Annual Report*, 2 (1880-1881): 80-81.

"The Seven Brothers of the Star Cluster," in *Seneca Myths and Folktales*, by Arthur C. Parker (Buffalo, NY: Buffalo Historical Society, 1923), 83-85.

"Onondaga Tale of the Pleiades," by W. M. Beauchamp, *Journal of American Folklore*, 13-14 (1900-1901): 281-82.

"How the Dancing Stars Got Into the Sky," in *Around an Iroquois Story Fire*, by Mabel Powers (NY: Frederick A. Stokes, 1923), 52-58.

"Oot-Kwah-Tah, the Seven Star Dancers," in *Keepers of the Night*, by Michael J. Caduto and Joseph Bruchac (Golden, CO: Fulcrum, 1994), 63-65.

The Dancing Stars: An Iroquois Legend, by Anne Rockwell (NY: Thomas Crowell, 1972).

The Turtle Who Couldn't Stop Talking

This story is found in *The Fables of Bidpai* and *The Kacchapa Jataka*. We adapted the ending to explain the turtle's cracked shell. Other sources we referred to are:

"The Turtle Who Could Not Stop Talking," in *In the Nursery of My Bookhouse*, edited by Olive Beaupre´ Miller (Chicago: The Bookhouse for Children, 1920), 238-41.

"The Talkative Tortoise," in *Indian Fairy Tales*, selected and edited by Joseph Jacobs (London: David Nutt, 1892), 100-02.

"The Talkative Tortoise," in *Stories to Tell to Children*, by Sara Cone Bryant (NY: Houghton Mifflin, 1907), 165-67.

The Story of Arachne

The Metamorphoses, Ovid (NY: Viking, 1958), 147-51.

Book of Greek Myths, by Ingri D'Aulaire and Edgar Parin D'Aulaire (Garden City, NY: Doubleday, 1962), 36.

"Arachne, the Eternal Spinner," in *The Firebringer and Other Great Stories*, by Louis Untermeyer (NY: M. Evans & Co., 1968), 38-40.

"The Spinning Contest," in *Classic Myths to Read Aloud*, by William F. Russell (NY: Crown, 1989), 64-67.

Rabbit Counts the Crocodiles

"The Counting of the Crocodiles," in *The Tiger's Whisker and Other Tales from Asia and the Pacific*, by Harold Courlander (NY: Harcourt Brace & World, 1959), 87-89.

"The White Hare and the Crocodiles," in *The Japanese Fairy Book*, by Yei Theodora Ozaki (Archibald Constable & Co., 1903 [reprinted by Dover, 1967]), 214-23.

"The Rabbit and the Crocodile," in *The Dancing Kettle and Other Japanese Folktales*, by Yoshiko Uchida (NY: Harcourt Brace & World, 1949), 49-57.

The Ugandan version we mentioned was told by a student at Tuskegee Institute named Daniel Mkato. It may be found in A.H. Faucet, "Negro Tales from the South," *Journal of American Folklore* 40 (1927): 224.

The Straw, the Coal, and the Bean

"The Straw, the Coal, and the Bean," in *More Tales from Grimm*, by Wanda Gag (NY: Coward-McCann, Inc., 1947), 95-98.

"The Straw, the Coal, and the Bean," in *Stories and Storytelling*, by Angela M. Keyes (NY: Appleton, 1911), 136-38.

"The Straw, the Coal, and the Bean," in *The Tall Book of Nursery Tales* (NY: Harper, 1944), 90-91.

How Brazilian Beetles Got Their Gorgeous Coats

"How the Brazilian Beetles Got their Gorgeous Coats," in *Fairy Tales from Brazil*, by Elsie Spicer Eells (NY: Dodd, Mead, 1917), 201-07.

"How Beetles Got Their Beautiful Coats," in *Folktales of Latin America*, by Shirlee P. Newman (NY: Bobbs-Merrill, 1962), 67-71.

The Quarrel

"Origin of Strawberries," in *Myths of the Cherokee*, by James Mooney, U.S. Bureau of American Ethnology, *Annual Report*, 19, pt. 1 (1897-98): 259.

The First Strawberries: A Cherokee Story, retold by Joseph Bruchac (NY: Dial, 1993).

John Rattling-Gourd of Big Cove: A Collection of Cherokee Legends, by Corydon Bell (NY: Macmillan, 1955), 22-26.

"The Strawberries," in *American Indian Tales and Legends*, by Vladimir Hulpach (London: Paul Hamlyn, 1965), 131-33.

Why Parrots Only Repeat What People Say

"The Bird that Told Tales," in *The Elephant's Bathtub: Wonder Tales from the Far East*, by Frances Carpenter (Garden City, NY: Doubleday, 1962), 58-65.

"Why the Parrot Repeats Man's Words," in *Ride With the Sun: Folktales and Stories from all Countries of the United Nations*, edited by Harold Courlander (NY: Whittlesey House, 1955), 34-37.

"The Lorikeet and Man," from *Tales from Thailand*, as told by Marian Davies Toth (Rutland, VT: Charles E. Tuttle, 1971), 166-68.

"Why the Parrot and the Minor Bird but Echo the Words of Man," in *Laos Folklore of Farther India*, by K.N. Fleeson (NY: Revell & Co., 1899), 41-44.

The Taxi Ride

"Why Do Dogs Chase Cars?" in *South and North, East and West: The Oxfam Book of Children's Stories*, edited by Michael Rosen (Cambridge, MA: Candlewick Press, 1992). Adapted by permission.

How Owl Got His Feathers

"The Plumage of the Owl," in *The Three Wishes: a Collection of Puerto Rican Folktales*, by Ricardo E. Alegria (NY: Harcourt Brace & World, 1969), 64-65. Adapted by permission.

Two Brothers, Two Rewards

"The Pumpkin Seeds," in *The Story Bag: a Collection of Korean Folktales*, by Kim So-Un (Rutland VT: Charles E. Tuttle, 1955), 145-53.

"The Man Who Cuts the Cinnamon Tree," in *Folktales of China*, by Lee Wyndham (NY: Bobbs-Merrill, 1963), 117-21.

Just Rewards, by Steve Sanfield (NY: Orchard Books, 1996).

"The Hurt Sparrow," in *Fairy Tales of the Orient* (Japanese variant), by Pearl S. Buck (NY: Simon & Schuster, 1965), 181-83.

Older Brother, Younger Brother: A Korean Folktale, retold by Nina Jaffe (NY: Viking, 1995).

"The Man in the Moon," in *Folktales of China*, by Eberhard Wolfram (Chicago: University of Chicago Press, 1965), 125-27.

Why Bear Has a Stumpy Tail

"Why the Bear is Stumpy-tailed" in *Popular Tales from the Norse*, by Peter Christian Asbjörnsen and Jorgen Moe, translated by George Webbe Dasent (NY: G.P. Putnam, 1882), 172.

Funk and Wagnall's Standard Dictionary of Folklore, Mythology, and Legend, edited by Maria Leach (NY: Funk & Wagnalls, 1949), 1: 126.

Where All Stories Come From

"The Coming of Legends," in *Iroquois Stories*, by Joseph Bruchac (Trumansburg, NY: Crossing Press, 1985).

"The Talking Stone," in *The Talking Stone: An Anthology of Native American Tales & Legends*, edited by Dorothy de Wit (NY: Greenwillow Books, 1979), 5-9.

"The Origin of Stories," in *Seneca Indian Myths*, by Jeremiah Curtin (NY: Dutton, 1923), 70-75.

"The Story of Hahskwahot," in "Seneca Fiction, Legends and Myths," by Jeremiah Curtin and J.N.B. Hewitt, U.S. Bureau of American Ethnology, *Annual Report* (1910-1911), 32: 680-81.

"The Legend of the Origin of All Legends," in *Owenah and Other Indian Stories*, adapted by William Heidt, Jr. (Ithaca, NY: DeWitt Historical Society, 1962), 19-21.